A Dog with No Tail

A Dog with No Tail

Hamdi Abu Golayyel

Translated by
Robin Moger

The American University in Cairo Press
Cairo New York

This paperback edition published in 2015 by
The American University in Cairo Press
113 Sharia Kasr el Aini, Cairo, Egypt
420 Fifth Avenue, New York, NY 10018
www.aucpress.com

Exclusive distribution outside Egypt and North America by I.B. Tauris & Co Ltd., 6 Salem Road, London, W4 2BU

Dar el Kutub No. 7554/15
ISBN 978 977 416 736 2

Dar el Kutub Cataloging-in-Publication Data

Abu Golayyel, Hamdi.
A Dog with No Tail / Hamdi Abu Golayyel; translated by Robin Moger.—Cairo: The American University in Cairo Press, 2015.
p. cm.
ISBN 978 977 416 736 2
1. English fiction
823

1 2 3 4 5 19 18 17 16 15

Designed by Andrea El-Akshar
Printed in Egypt

Some people carry spare change and some don't . . . thus is life.

—Ibrahim Mansour

I believe that what happened to me happens to every human being in exactly the same way.

—Marguerite Duras

I Keep the Files Stored in My Head, My Friend

I smoked the joint. It was strong. I say that about every joint I smoke—that it's strong, that it's "good stuff"—but this one seemed particularly potent. One piece of hash makes five perfect cigarettes. If I'd been with friends I would've made eight, even ten, but instead I made just three. Convinced myself it would help me think about the novel. I rolled each one differently and told myself each time: I'll start with this one.

I always seem to start with the weakest, the worst. Some flaw in my make-up means I never do better than good endings. I lack the trick of picking the best things first. If I have two books, I'll start with the one I think inferior. When I sit down to eat I plan things out so that my last mouthful is the morsel I crave. I'm one of those people who saves the choicest cuts till last. This joint was the weakest. Number two in the rolling sequence. I'd rolled one before it and one after it.

As I made the first joint I'd been dying for the hash: craving the little crumbs as they trickled into the mouth of the cigarette. For the second (the middle) joint, I was overcome by sudden circumspection. I was, let's say, tight-fisted. It's not like falling off a log, after all. No mean feat for a man to get a bit of space to himself and start rolling.

The last joint was pure hash. The heaviest hash crumbs get lost in the mix and end up being poured into the last joint.

But this one would do the job. Reducing the amount of tobacco is a good idea. It was the sort of stuff that left you feeling at peace with yourself, that the world still lay before you. The fact that I'm currently wandering around my room is the most overt symptom of my enjoyment of quality product.

Thoughts shake me nearly to pieces.

At times like these I picture my life as files stored away in my head. Sometimes they unfold one by one, but sometimes they all spill open at once and childhood memories are jumbled up with the image of the last face I've seen. Right now, I'm seeing myself in Shubra. I was twenty, just returned from a stint working in Libya, and employed as a manual laborer while I looked for a job. I lived in a room in Ain Shams with four guys from the village. I was working for a demolition contractor. No, not demolition: demolition and construction.

He only worked with houses on the verge of collapse. The places sealed up with red wax, directives issued to tear them down: these were his bread and butter. Peeling back the wax with a delicacy befitting its official status he would slip into the house with his men: one team to dig out the foundations and another to smash down pillars and walls. A few days later and the miracle is complete: the decaying pile has become a lofty, freshly painted tower. Most of the old houses in Shubra and the surrounding neighborhoods owed their continued existence to him.

I worked with the utmost diligence and devotion and he made me his favorite, privileging me over the others on the grounds that I "worked like a donkey" and "my eyes never left the ground." In 1992, as the earthquake struck Cairo, I was digging at the bottom of a foundation trench beneath a three-story house, but everyone, even those closest to me, were left in no doubt that I was first and foremost a journalist. The stories I'd had published were enlisted to support my claims that I was, in fact, an editor for the *al-Ahrar* newspaper, which, I reckoned, was just about credible for someone in my position.

Sometimes I'd say I was continuing my studies. If anyone asked what I was studying I'd panic. Then I learned of something called The Institute of Literary Criticism, and struck by the grandeur of the name I started claiming that I studied there. All the while I was hunting for a job, any job: reputable employment, starting at eight in the morning and finishing at two in the afternoon. I applied to hundreds of ministries, companies, and offices all over Cairo, and on one occasion to a cultural institute. A friend from the village and I came across an advertisement, placed by the august Association, for a cultural official.

"Let's see it then, Mr. Author," said my companion.

And we went. It wasn't far: the selection committee's headquarters were a couple of stops from the café. The examiner was an elderly man, his body corpulent and his hair frizzy and bright white. A little placard inscribed with his name and position perched on the desk.

In my experience, it was the done thing to interview us individually, but for some reason he made us stand in single file facing him: me, my companion, and about eight other graduates. His desk was vast. He seemed to be searching for something relevant to ask us. I later recalled, perhaps I imagined it, that his office was cluttered with cassette tapes. I was first in line. My friend had pushed me to the front, for reasons that will become clear later, and I now stood directly opposite the examiner. He sprawled ostentatiously behind his desk as we jostled and bumped, clearly unconvinced that any of us were suited for the position, and conducted the examination with the apathy of one who knows the result in advance. He looked at me unenthusiastically, and abruptly announced,

"I've faith in you, my pretty,
That you'd keep the secret I told . . . ."

Before this could sink in, he snapped,

"Whose words are those?"

I burst out laughing. I had heard this song a number of times—I even hummed it to myself on occasion—but I never expected to hear it from the mouth of so exalted a personage. The way he drew out the song in a brutal warble then suddenly whirled around to surprise, or rather assault, me with his question was something I was unable to let pass in silence. I tried to apologize. I almost kissed his hands. I told him I was from the countryside, that I had just remembered something funny, but he insisted on canceling the meeting. My interview, and with it those of my friend and the other applicants, was at an end.

But for that fatuous cackle I would've become a distinguished cultural official. I was the best candidate: I had brought a file of my published work. Let's have no regrets. It had nothing to with laughter. I have a fear of such things, of taking down files, standing in queues, respecting one's elders and betters. They're demeaning. I feel as though I'm begging. Construction work was easier and I figured I'd be no good at anything else. Sometimes I think I'm interested in writing for the same reason. Naturally, I love to succeed—to excel—but I have no faith in my abilities. Success comes at a high price, and writing helps me avoid paying it. It seems my faculties of expression have let me down as usual. Nevertheless, I would like to say that writing lets me take pride in myself, even as I lug sacks of earth around. Just the thought that I've penned stories puts everything to rights.

But I must get back to the point . . . . So I mentioned that these things help me think about the novel. But which novel? Five years now and I flit from one to another. I begin a novel, grow fond of it, the pages pile up effortless and uncomplicated, and suddenly a new tale reveals itself . . . .

I must go back to my grandfather. My grandfather Aula: the first story, the first tale, of my life. He lived until the 1950s, one of the first Bedouin tribesmen to settle in the Southern Fayoum and abandon his life of prowling and plundering. In his youth he carried a twelve-bore shotgun and led a band of armed men to abduct, plunder, and wreak vengeance on the enemy on behalf of the tribe, in the days when one man would dispatch two or three of his foes single-handed. Today, legends abound of his killing sprees and his victims. It's said he was an honest man: he'd murder and steal, sure, but he told people the truth to their faces and never lied. It's also said he was jinxed. He couldn't creep into a home or sneak into a field without being discovered. As he used to say himself, "The job I turn up for is doomed." When the tribes settled and the government began to tighten its grip, he built himself a room on the edge of the desert that stretched from South Fayoum to Aswan and called it his office. He laid a mat outside and sat down to wait. In mere days it had become a mecca for all. Everyone who had stolen livestock in northern Upper Egypt came there to hide it, and everyone who had had livestock stolen in northern Upper Egypt came there to get it back in exchange for a commission received by Aula and passed on to the thieves.

Of course, in the beginning the office worked in secret and Aula had to hide the animals in the fields and mountains, but in no time at all it was operating quite openly, recognized by the government as a sort of security agency whose appointed task was the restitution of property to its rightful owners. One night, thieves made off with sheep belonging to Abdullah Abu Mansour, my grandfather's cousin, one of the first people from the area to have attended a government school, and a lawyer. He was renowned for his sharp tongue and bizarre appearance, entering the village wearing a suit and riding a bicycle.

He spoke with a city accent and treated his relatives and neighbors like wild animals.

Out of respect for the bonds of kinship, Aula visited him at home and told him, "Your sheep are with me and they're safe. Though most people pay ten, you'll pay five . . . ." At this the lawyer rose up and screamed, "Thief! Moron! You think this country's still the mess it used to be? I'll ruin you!" then marched straight to the police station, unfurled his judicial honorifics, and filed a complaint against "Aula Abu Mansour Raslan Abu Golayyel for stealing livestock and disturbing the peace." A unit sallied forth from the station, arrested my grandfather Aula, and threw him into jail, and the lawyer swaggered back to the village. But that very night, or thereabouts, thieves made off with livestock from a house next to the station. They searched everywhere, down to the ditches and the cracks in the ground, but not a trace of the animals was found. The superintendent had no choice but to release Aula.

"Can you get them for me?" he asked.

"Yes," Aula replied and left.

The next day the sheep were found tied to the station window.

I feel a file opening.

Whenever I stumble a file seems to open.

It's my file on writers, or, let's say, on authors. There's always an author in this file, some novelist who sends me into raptures, who is, I sense, writing about me. I start out by imitating him, but eventually he cedes his place in the file to another novelist and I begin to exact my revenge. I have no idea why I take such pleasure in revenging myself on the writers I admire. A while back there was an author (no need to mention his name) whom I felt I knew personally. He used this conceit of a murderer and the victim's voice. I can't be sure that I'm remembering this correctly, but I seem to recall a room, and a telephone sitting between the murderer and his victim. The victim sprawls on the bed as the murderer calmly ponders the crime he has just committed. And suddenly, there's the sound of a telephone ringing . . . . It rings three times before the answering machine engages and the victim's voice issues forth with the familiar message:

"I'm not at home at the moment. Please call another time."

Dreams

The Doctor dreams methodically: every so often he is visited by a new dream. All his dreams come true. What are all the jobs he's done but dreams come true? He doesn't overreach himself, though. He has no desire to turn his life upside down; he merely seeks to improve his circumstances. Rolling in the dust of the building trade he dreamt of guarding trucks. Rather than spend sleepless nights guarding trucks he dreamt of traveling the country as a driver's mate. Instead of dozing before a garage of heavy-goods trucks he dreamt of his backside on the comfy bench outside the actress' building. And this was his greatest dream of all.

His name was Shinhabi, but he always felt the need to explain that "it's Sinhabi on my ID card." The medical moniker dated from his days in the pharmacy. He'd always had that strong body, the pale skin, and the green eyes, and when he took the time and cleaned himself up, you'd think him quite the gentleman. People who met him for the first time would be completely taken in. They wouldn't bat an eye to hear him called "Doctor." A perfectly shrewd friend of mine saw him in our village clad in a white gallabiya and suede jacket and thought he was a government vet.

The Doctor went to Cairo young. His father died and he didn't continue his education. He dropped out in his second year of high school, but he would have left even if his father had lived. His father had tuberculosis and not much else, aside from a mat to sleep on, a blanket, and two rooms with reeds for a roof. I knew him toward the end of his life: a thin robe wrapped around a hunched skeleton. I would see him every day, rolling out a cigarette as he perched on the mound in the middle of our village. It was said that the cigarettes loosened him up and I got the habit from him. To this day I won't enter the bathroom without my cigarette.

The Doctor was quick to get his affairs in order. He went off to work with his Nubian cousins on the work gangs all over Cairo and stayed at his aunt's buildings in al-Waili. Together with her Upper Egyptian husband she had been looking after a villa for an ancient Englishman, and when he died it went to her. She joined forces with her sisters' children, who lived back in the village, and in place of the old villa erected a tall, gaudily painted building. But the Doctor had no time for the way his cousins made their living. It didn't sit right with him, so he went off to earn his living at the daily laborers' markets on the public squares and bridges: the first person from our village to discover Shubra and Mi'allim Matar's crew. His unshakably rude health qualified him to carry sand, gravel, cement, and tiles. He could lift two meters of red bricks and carry them to the top of the highest building in Egypt. Working alongside him in Bousta almost killed me. He was also the first person from our village to work as a loader for goods trucks, as a driver's mate, wiping down cars, hawking videotapes, and as a doorman.

Over the course of successive generations, the young men of our village have, without exception, made their way to Shubra. More than mere job hunting, it's something like a local tradition, a first step that every man must take at the start of his life: independence, self-reliance, and returning to the village with a few hard-earned pennies. Once a man has developed the beginnings of a mustache and a sense of self-worth, he travels to Shubra. For my generation the trip was an adventure for the brave and the bold. To miss out was to court disparagement of your intelligence and open-mindedness: your ability to pass beyond the limits of your world.

And every one of them, educated and unlettered alike, worked as manual laborers (the most contemptible and, by a considerable margin, the toughest of the professions) yet they were ashamed to work as doormen, loaders, and drivers' mates, or even as craftsmen in the construction gangs. He'd carry dirt but he wouldn't work, that was the boast. However, when circumstances forced one of us into this life of labor, he'd do his best to conceal it from his very closest relatives. I myself would put in two or three weeks' hard graft in Shubra, and on my return to the village tried my best to convince people that I was, in fact, a pilot in Cairo. For the entire holiday I would assume the mantle of village intellectual. Rising late, towel slung over my shoulder, I would make my way down to the canal bank, with my toothbrush and toothpaste—the proofs of cultivation, culture, and an upward social trajectory—borne aloft.

The Doctor wasn't ashamed. He worked lots of different jobs. He cleaned cars, distributed videotapes, and traveled the length and breadth of the country as a truck driver's mate. Yet he never stayed in one occupation for long. He'd dream of a job for months, years even, familiarize himself with its smallest details, and finally decide that it was there, and there alone, that his future lay; a final solution to the grubbing around and ignominy he suffered in the building trade. He'd move mountains to get the work, but after a while, when he'd gotten so good at it you'd think he'd been born to it, boredom set in and he would turn his mind to another dream.

When he got hold of the night guard job we had just started working in Shubra. We were commuting workers, a little more respectable than usual, traveling up to Cairo, staying a while, then returning to the village. We knew nothing of Cairo beyond Ahmed Helmi Square, Salim's café, and the buildings where Mi'allim Matar's crew worked. We would sleep in the buildings or, when the mi'allim owed us wages, in his red Mazda pickup licensed for transporting workers. Usually there were no more than five or six of us, mostly from the village of Daniel in the Itsa Fayoum municipality. The Doctor, by virtue of age and experience, was our leader. We were all studying: he was the only one with time on his hands. He would sleep in the buildings, sit with us at the café, and trail after Matar. But he also turned his attention to the shops and stores, the homes and streets, hunting down the daily wage and the daily grind, working one day and sleeping ten. One morning, standing on the corner of Muniyat al-Seirig Street, he found the solution. An agency for heavy-goods vehicles was looking for a night guard. We used to walk the entire length of Muniyat al-Seirig to reach Salim's café before the crew bosses left. The agency specialized in cement trucks. Its vehicles went everywhere from Alexandria to Aswan. It was a modest little place and spattered with motor oil. At first glance you would think it was a workshop, but in his dreams the Doctor saw it as a means to escape the misery of day labor. Whenever we passed by he'd stop us in the middle of the street and then it would be, "If only everybody could get work like this. I swear to God it's the real deal. A fixed salary at the start of every month and on top of that, you're only working at night. The day is yours: sleep, work, run around the streets, it's up to you . . . ."

One fine day, I, the Doctor, and two guys from back home read a notice pasted on the metal door: WANTED: NIGHT GUARD FOR GOODS VEHICLES.

The agency's office wasn't open and no guard was in evidence so we waited and eventually someone appeared. The Doctor stepped forward, kissed his cheeks, and greeted him.

The garage owned about five large cabs and their trailers. Some went out transporting their loads around the country and the others stayed parked out front. The Doctor's task was to guard the parked trucks at night and his place of work was located beneath one of them. Every day, running up to the café to catch the bosses before they left, we would come across him yawning and stretching as he emerged from under a truck. As soon as he had started the Doctor devised a plan to improve his lot. Instead of staying awake all night guarding the trucks, he found a way to sleep.

Muniyat al-Seirig Street, especially in the direction of Dawaran Shubra, was home to wild dogs that passed their daylight hours sunk in a deep sleep with forepaws outstretched. The Doctor put them to use. Each night he would beg a bunch of chicken legs from the poultry vendor on the corner. He'd tie them to a plastic bag, or a sheet of cardboard, or any old piece of paper so long as it was rough, then he'd place them beside his head and lie down. The moment he sensed movement in the street, he would stretch out his hand, half-asleep, and shake the legs. He'd ring them like a bell. Every dog in the street would set off toward him, barking their heads off, and swarm around the truck where he slept, a cacophonous canine riot terrifying to passing citizens. The passersby would take to their heels before they were devoured, the Doctor would replace the chicken legs, and the dogs would trot away.

And so it would go until morning. It only took a few days for the dogs to adjust and develop a firm bond with the Doctor. They knew exactly what was expected of them. The instant they sniffed out a passing shadow their voices would rise heavenward and they would descend upon him, at which point the Doctor would come to the rescue. Truth be told, he exploited this state of affairs in the worst possible way. He purposefully delayed his interventions, thus ensuring the passersby were frightened out of their wits. Just picture yourself for a moment, walking alone at the dead of night, suddenly confronted with an army of dogs attacking you from every side. The neighborhood was shaken to the core. Its residents were of one mind when it came to the danger of walking in the street after ten at night. And the Doctor slept. He slept and snored, making up for all those lost days and months. Those places where once he couldn't find a place to take a shit, much less lay his head, were now his and his alone. He could sleep anywhere and it was his right.

And when he'd glutted himself on sleep he began to cast his eye over the street. He noticed that across from his spot by the trucks, and stretching the length of the street, was a long line of cars. Asking no one's advice, and forgoing idle hours at Salim's café, he took up his rag and, recklessly putting his faith in the maxim that "no man can ignore you if you've cleaned his car for a month," he set to. By the time the sun had risen he'd polished off every car in the street. He cleaned up; he flourished; he grew fat. His reputation spread through the street and the neighborhood. Even his nights changed. Instead of sleeping courtesy of street dogs he began to spend happy hours prying into the lives of his neighbors, and in doing so he revived an old tradition. Back in the village we used to take great pleasure spying on newlyweds (Bedouin or peasant, it didn't matter) on their wedding night. We would creep up to their windows and watch everything, spending countless delightful evenings at the invitation of the Doctor. Directly opposite the office lay the apartment of a peculiar married couple. By day he was a respectable man of influence and she a lady of good repute, but by night? A complete farce. They had sex—extremely violent sex—every single day. I watched them once (well, several times), and was utterly unable to hold myself together, going to pieces as he, haughty and pompous, pressed on.

For some months the Doctor divided his life between guarding trucks and wiping cars, but the owner of the agency started to cramp his style. He confronted him about the car cleaning and warned him several times against taking liberties. Better he look to his job lest he send him back to the building trade. Then he gave him another responsibility: guard the trucks by night and wash them during the day. One morning, just as the Doctor was packing away his bedding from under a parked truck, an articulated truck from Suez pulled in and the driver's mate got down. He was swaying where he stood; off his face and a beer bottle in his hand. The Doctor quickly weighed his options: the owner couldn't stand him, and anyone who could drink to the point of inebriation was certainly earning more than a car guard who scarcely had enough to eat. Wasting no time he brought it up with the owner.

"I want to work in a cab."

"What, a driver's mate?"

"Yes."

"Right, and you know all about that, do you? You've done it before?"

"If you want to learn, you'll learn . . . ."

"I'm finding it hard to employ you as a guard. I tell myself you're having it tough and you need the work. But because of that silver tongue of yours I'll take you on as a driver's mate. If you can do it, you can do it. If you're no good, show me your back and I don't want to see you around here again."

The Doctor vanished from the street. He left without telling a soul. The head of the agency informed me with relish, "He took off on a cement truck heading to Aswan."

A Private Job

I sat in the center of what remained of the pile of sand. It lay in a circle around me. I squatted and looked up. I had climbed to the top of that building and down again one hundred and forty times. Seven floors, two apartments to a floor. The residents were cooperative. They gave me glasses of iced water all day. They saw how it was when a sack spilled onto the stairs. It was heavy. I couldn't climb up to the roof with it and fling it down. It was the first time I had moved a complete load of sand on my own. From the outset I preferred working with sand. Sand is cleaner. All I had to do was bathe and not a single piece of evidence that I was a day laborer would remain. Then there's the fact that you can lie in bed for a week on the cost of unloading a whole van of sand.

You lean over the sack and gently brush it clean. Then you hug it to you, opening your legs to accommodate it, while your chest gets ready to suck in double the air. You hold it steady with your forearm. You rest for a moment. You breathe in, say "Ho!" or "Uff!" and heave it onto your shoulder.

I normally worked using a relay system. I'd join three or four laborers and we would divide up the building, each man climbing a floor or two and handing it on to his colleague. This was the first time I'd worked like this, carrying a sack from the ground floor to the roof. A meter of sand is exactly twenty sacks, and a sack weighs sixty kilos. I lifted seven meters to the roof on the seventh floor. To this day I consider it a miracle.

I was late. I arrived at the café at about nine o'clock, ordered tea, and got the news from Salim. Everybody, laborers and skilled workers alike, had left with Mi'allim Matar to shore up a building in Gazirat Badran. I thought of going after them. Gazirat Badran (which is, incidentally, famous for the number of Syrians living there: its best known street is called Palaces of the Syrians) was only a short walk away and Matar wouldn't mind: he'd find me enough work to make up for the hour I missed. But I was lazy, or rather, I was embarrassed: it is unbecoming to impose oneself. Matar saw me all the time and if he needed men he'd call on me. I began to ready myself for a wasted day. I thought about what I wanted to do and found that it was nothing in particular. I live in Ain Shams, I work as a manual laborer, and I wait. I weighed my options—Amm Ahmed's tea stall in Tahrir and a literary gathering in Giza—and plumped for Amm Ahmed. The conference wasn't for a few hours yet and if I wanted to I could go after visiting Amm Ahmed. Groping in my pocket for change to pay for my tea, I considered heading straight over to the Sheikh Ramadan bus stop, but I told myself to wait a while. A private employer walked in. I knew them by the way they moved: cautious, hesitant, and haughty all at the same time. They were known as private employers because they came from outside the building trade. Ordinary people. Savvy clerks and nine-to-fivers who prefer to repair or even build their houses themselves. On the whole their jobs are easy: repairs, breaking up a kitchen or bathroom, carrying furniture downstairs . . . that kind of thing. They would treat us like guests, take care of us all day, and pay generous rates. I used to shy away from working with them. It was out of embarrassment. We'd work in people's homes, in the midst of families. I'd spend all day trying to make them see that I wasn't how they imagined. I'd be working as a manual laborer and having them understand that I wasn't one, supporting my claims with erudite turns of phrase of the kind spouted by lovers of culture and learning. Sometimes I'd recite poetry:

"The heart fluttered in my side like a slaughtered cock,
O heart be still! I cried,
Then my tears and the wounded past replied,
'Why did we return? Would that we had not!'"

or:

"You are, and I am, and my heart suffers not through
My longing for you, nor do my eyes grow dry.
When my soul confides to you, despair and grief
Might make an end of me
But for this, my solace, my relief."

Some of the clients got annoyed and some acted as if they quite understood.

The private client I'd waited for was tall and wore a green safari suit. When Salim started singing my praises I did my best to appear otherwise occupied. I stared at the ground, I gazed out at the street, I said hello to a passing stranger. Waiting for these people put me on edge. I, too, was a private citizen and one of these days I'd have a proper job. Salim told him I worked like a donkey; that I was well-mannered; that my eyes never left the ground. He nodded his head, satisfied, and came over. Toward me came the private client.

"You're a laborer?"

"No," I declared to myself, and would have said it out loud if he hadn't butted in.

"It's a load of sand: seven meters. You'll carry it up to the seventh floor. Do what you want. If you want to do it yourself, go ahead. If you want to contract it out and bring a couple of other guys with you, I don't mind."

I instantly loathed him and resolved to overcharge him: if he agreed, he agreed. If he didn't he could go to hell.

"A meter's seven pounds," I said, "and seven sevens make forty-seven."

"You mean forty-nine. Plus a pound from me makes it a square fifty."

I wavered between delight at his generosity and resentment at his generosity and regretted not charging him more. I followed him out. We passed by Sheikh Ramadan mosque, negotiated a puddle, and stopped in at a building supplier's where we bought sacks. About fifty or sixty of the empty, white cement sacks. I used to like them best of all: white, clean, and made of paper panels that were easy on the shoulder. They absorbed sweat, they didn't get soggy too easily, and they could hold about twice as much as the regular sacks.

I picked them up, these fifty or sixty sacks folded under my arm, and we entered a narrow street, coming to a halt in front of the sand pile. He pointed out the roof on the seventh floor, cautioned me against disturbing the neighbors, handed over fifty pounds, and left.

Hamdi

The craftsmen in Matar's crew were mostly from around Muniyat al-Seirig and Shubra. Sometimes they would be joined by guys from provinces in the north and south, but they'd drive them off, hassling them and treating them with contempt until they left. I didn't like to work with them. Easy though it was to work with a plasterer, a tiler, or a plumber, I preferred carrying sand, gravel, and cement to working with them. Even mixing the cement was better. They were—without exception and completely without provocation—foul-mouthed: "faggot" this, "pimp" that, and so on.

Still, I made friends with one of them. He was a skimmer and I worked with him for ages. In the morning, I'd go straight around to his room near the café and we'd breakfast on hot felafel with tahina, smoke a couple of cigarettes, and go off to work, either at one of Matar's buildings or a repair job he'd managed to sneak on the side. It was a pleasure to work with him, something between a holiday and a comedy. Firstly, he was extremely lazy. The plaster he managed to adhere to the wall was nothing compared to the amount he spattered over his face and clothes and into his eyes. The boss never used him except in cramped, out-of-the-way spots where the customers weren't so bothered about the quality of the work, and where skill was less important than an ability to wriggle into small places (if they were stifling, all the better) like bathrooms, kitchens, basements, and stairwells. I'd mix him up a single sack of cement. The quota for a halfway-talented skimmer in a well-run crew like Mi'allim Mata's was five sacks and a single four-walled room in a day. He would splash and muddle around in a single sack-worth, wouldn't finish it, and I'd have to bury what was left somewhere far from the eyes of Matar.

The first thing that drew me to him was his name. A strange name; obscure and unintelligible. I once expressed how I felt about it in a short story. It wasn't Hamad or Haamed or Hamid, but Hamdi. You didn't know whether it referred to you or the person you were talking to. Most of the Hamdis I've known have either been crackpots or idiots of some kind. Hamdi our neighbor in the village was a freak. He had a huge penis. They said he could rest its tip on the ground when he pissed. Now, it's a matter of common knowledge that the well-endowed are prone to mental instability. It's not so clear, however, if this claim is motivated by spite and revenge or possibly a desire to affirm that a shortness of appendage (a problem that has haunted men down the ages) is in fact a natural state, or whether the long-dongs really are insane or at least soft in the head. The other Hamdi I knew from primary and secondary school was definitely crazy. He was called Hamdi the Fool and he used to admit it of himself. This one time he stopped me on the street, put his hand on my shoulder and, with spittle flecking my face, declared, "Hamdi the Fool says to you, 'Your mother's cunt.'"

He terrified me. This was in the fifties. He would dribble in his beard and ride around on a stalk of wheat or a sunflower like it was a car, honking his horn, swerving, and hitting the brakes to save people and passing sheep.

At first, when I'd see Hamdi Shadid at the café I'd think of Hung Hamdi and Hamdi the Fool and make a quick comparison. He was closer to Hamdi the Fool in shape: his bulk, his stammer, and his unkempt beard. It wasn't long or short, just the beard of someone who wasn't doing so well. But his reserve and contentment with his lot reminded me of Hung Hamdi.

Though he often earned his living as a skimmer he didn't restrict himself. He did everything: a laborer and a skilled worker rolled up in one. If it could be carried he'd carry it, and he knew what he was about: he went out each morning to get his wage and he'd come back each evening with the money in his pocket.

The Story of My Family

I've tried to write the story of my family many times, but I always fail, and here I am failing in front of you as we speak. It's an interesting subject—tragedies, miracles, and myths—but then I hesitate and lose my nerve. The first complicating factor is the sheer number of them. There are distinct differences between the different branches. They range in color from white-skinned as a European to black as an African. Then there's the fact that as a breed they are irritable and talkative and generally impossible to please. In 1997 I wrote a maudlin story about the family martyr, Muawwad Abu Golayyel, the lieutenant colonel assassinated during the Palestinian uprising in Rafah, and they went ballistic. One of them actually began legal proceedings against me. Many of them cut me off. Some refuse to greet me to this day. So, taking refuge from such complications and sharp tongues, and not forgetting, of course, my anticipated failure, I will confine myself to history. Facts agreed on by all. Maybe they will encourage me (and even better, encourage you) to deal with that which bashfulness and want of talent prevent me revealing.

The Abu Golayyel family are al-Rimah Bedouin, and it's claimed that they are descended from al-Fawayid Bedouin such as Judge Badir of the Sira Hilaliya, the epic saga of the Hilal tribe. Interestingly, some of them resemble old Badir, especially when it comes to meanness, cowardice, and shiftiness. My mother describes one of my uncles as a catfish. "He's slippery," she says. "You can't get a hold on him."

The family's made up of nine "houses," or branches, based in nine small villages strung out over a three-kilometer stretch of the Southern Fayoum, with the last village in line sitting on the edge of the desert that divides the Fayoum from the governorates of Minya and Beni Suef. Seven of these villages bear the name Abu Golayyel and owe allegiance to his descendants. These are, in order, Atiya Abu Golayyel, Mohamedain Abu Golayyel, Abd al-Qawi Abu Golayyel, Sultan Abu Golayyel, Abd al-Ghani Abu Golayyel, Miftah Abu Golayyel, and Saqr Abu Golayyel. Six of the family's branches are entitled to, or own, the position of village headman. Some of them actually exercise their authority while others, having acquired the position at some point in the past, are content merely to bask in its prestige.

Incidentally, the family's headmen are poor and in bad shape, more like the guards of the headmen you see in TV dramas. One of them still furnishes his house with nothing but reed mats. Three of them were once famous among the Bedouin tribes of Libya and Egypt: Headman Abd al-Halim who mediated in the Libyan tribe disputes in the 1970s, back when the armed conflict between Sadat and Colonel Muammar al-Qadhafi was at its fiercest; Headman Ali Abu Yusif, brother of Dr. Abu Bakr Yusif, translator of a selection of Anton Chekhov's works and editor of translations of Dostoyevsky; and finally, Headman Abd al-Hamid Abd al-Raziq, author of a lengthy elegy to President Gamal Abd al-Nasser.

The overwhelming majority of the family are penniless, barely scraping by. Its young men work as doormen and guards in the modern tower blocks and apartment buildings of Cairo, particularly the neighborhoods of Faisal and Haram. I myself work as a laborer in and around Shubra. You can count the number of well-off Abu Golayyels on the fingers of one hand. Still, there are a lot of them. In numerical terms it's the largest Bedouin tribe in the Fayoum. Abu Golayyel the Elder sired nine, the nine produced tens, the tens hundreds and so on unto the fifth generation, which happens to be mine. My name in full: Hamdi Abu Hamed Eissa Saqr Abu Golayyel. Our ancestor came from Libya and made his way to Beheira, lived alongside the Awlad Ali in the deserts of Matrouh, before traveling to Sharqiya. Family legend asserts that the town of Kafr Saqr in Sharqiya is named for Saqr, the eldest of Abu Golayyel's sons.

He ended up in the Southern Fayoum, victim of a displacement policy designed to settle the Bedouin and bring an end to their peregrinations and interminable raids against the granaries and villages of the peasants. The displacement was decreed at the outset of the foundation of modern Egypt by Mohamed Ali Pasha, who took a number of measures to ensure the Bedouin did not rebel against him, such as granting them tax-exempt agricultural land and freeing all Bedouin men from the obligation of military service. This last measure is known in the history books as the "Arab Exception," and it remained in force until Gamal Abd al-Nasser abolished it in 1954. The first member of the family to join the army was born in 1935.

However, Mohamed Ali Pasha had another reason for keeping the Bedouin out of his army, something closer to fear and mistrust. Prior to his rule the Bedouin had fought with the Mamluk princes, not as regular troops, but as a seasoned cavalry force, waging war for personal gain. All historians of the French conquest mention these veterans, who were among the fiercest opponents of the campaign. The historian J. Christopher Herold, author of *Bonaparte in Egypt*, states that the French force in Alexandria separated into two divisions, or armies, the first making its way to the city of Rosetta and the second to Damietta. The army that went to Rosetta was met with drums and horns and endless nights of revelry. The division headed for Damietta ran into the Bedouin tribes. It was a mighty host, stretching out in a vast column of cannon, caravans, men, and livestock. The Bedouin cavalry faced them in a column of their own, fifty or sixty horsemen raiding this huge invading force from every direction, and as they darted about snatching up weapons, supplies, and baggage they also spirited away live soldiers and women. Christopher Herold writes with astonishment that the Bedouin treated the women with great dignity, leaving them in the tents with their honor intact while they went off to sleep with the men. They raped them senseless. He relates, with dry amusement, that one of these captured soldiers managed to find his way back to Bonaparte, but in a dreadful state. The supreme commander asked him what had happened but he just hung his head and stayed silent. "Speak up!" his leader bellowed at him, "Did they bugger you?"; at which he collapsed in floods of tears. Mohamed Ali couldn't be sure of them. He feared their ancient loyalties and the fact that they were incapable of being organized into a modern regular army.

To be honest I don't know that much about Abu Golayyel the Elder. I have no idea how he looked or acted and none of those who saw him alive survived to my time. However, I do know that he was an orphan. His father died, was perhaps killed, when he was an infant and he was given the nickname Abu Hazina, an allusion to his mother, Hazina. As is the custom of the Bedouin he was much older when he got the name Abu Golayyel, which was derived from the word jilal, a woolen cloak resembling the North African djellaba. It is said that once, as a boy, shaking from the cold, he cried out, "Mother, give me the jilal!" and from that day forth the name stuck.

So Abu Golayyel settled in the Southern Fayoum. His share from the Arab Exception was three hundred feddans of the finest agricultural land, but he never once planted it. He treated it as pasture and spent his life wandering around with his camels and sheep. A census of Bedouin in the region, conducted in 1854, describes him as a Bedouin chieftain, eighty-four years of age, with nine sons, the youngest of whom, Khalifa, was a year old.

I have heard two accounts of why he left (or to be precise: why he left Libya). The first concerns the climate—the drought then ravaging the Libyan highlands. The second hints at disgrace, an obscure transgression, whose punishment was exile. The Bedouin tribes have been imposing this punishment since before the coming of Islam. The chieftains and elders gather together and pass sentence to banish an individual. Abu Golayyel's descendants still enforce it against their neighbors to this day. They tell a person or a household to "get your belongings and get out" if they have shown disrespect or committed a particularly grievous sin.

Abu Golayyel came to the Fayoum as a young man. He went straight to al-Basil, an al-Rimah Bedouin like himself and a man of standing and influence. He owned a hundred feddans of land and held the chieftainship of all the Bedouin tribes in the Southern Fayoum. He took a liking to the young exile and married him to his daughter, Ghalia, who was Hamad Pasha al-Basil's aunt on his father's side. She gave birth to Abu Golayyel's eldest sons, Saqr, Raslan, and Deifullah, then he took another wife, a peasant woman from Tarsa, who gave him the rest of his nine sons. The grandchildren of the three elder brothers—Ghalia's children—still assert their superiority over descendants of the other six, offspring of the peasant, and insult their uncles. Unfortunately, it was the peasant's line that did well. While they amassed hundreds of feddans of land and occupied all the influential government positions, Ghalia's descendants (my family on both my mother's and father's side) are nonentities almost to a man.

The story of Abu Golayyel's marriage to Ghalia al-Basil is treated by their descendants as a historical fact beyond all dispute. Members of the al-Basil family, however, are more likely to cast doubt on it or, at the very least, never to have heard it. When I questioned the late Abu Bakr al-Basil, Member of Parliament for our constituency in the Fayoum and former head of parliament's agricultural committee, on the subject, he acted as if he were hearing about it for the first time. It was only embarrassment that made him say, "It's not, perhaps, entirely unlikely . . . ." What is certain is that when Hamad Pasha al-Basil returned from an exile shared with Saad Zaghloul he stopped in at Yasin Abu Golayyel's hideout; and that Abu Golayyel's direct descendents stormed the police stations and destroyed the railway line during the revolution of 1919 for no other reason than to avenge their cousin. It is also a fact that Aula Abu Raslan whipped and bound the police station's commanding officer with his reins, that another was martyred by English bullets, that six more were arrested and sent to prison where they wrote poetry, and that Yasin Abu Mahmoud was a Member of Parliament when it defied the English and met at the Shepheard Hotel in Cairo after the occupying authorities had decreed its dissolution. There's a family legend that claims the film *There's a Man in Our House* was about him. And it's true that he was just like the hero: he escaped the clutches of the political police during the revolution and took refuge with a Cairene family from Sayyida Zeinab, marrying their daughter and producing two sons.

I Reach Out My Hand and Blush that My Hand Reaches Out

As the first shocks of the 1992 earthquake hit I was in a pit, two meters square and a meter and a half deep, in the foundations of a dilapidated house. The Doctor was with me as I dug, filled the bucket, and handed it to him to be emptied on the tip outside. Down in the foundation trench, I felt none of the tremors that shook the rest of the nation. I labored on diligently as, over my head, people fled death.

I was also embarking on a sentimental adventure. I am peculiarly unable to endure the rejection of girls, a fear I confront by keeping my love secret and ignoring them, by skipping the whole drawn-out process and disdaining what I know to be unattainable. Down in the depths of that house I embarked on an adventure to suit my circumstances.

The house was the property of a married couple I recall with all the fondness in the world. At the end of the day you have to appreciate anyone who thinks you'd make a good match for his daughter.

To them I was no common laborer; I was a catch. The wife in particular got worked up over the idea of me as Struggling Youth, something the Doctor encouraged with stories about my situation in life and my education. Truth be told, I was quite happy to be seen like this, but at the same time I was unwilling to sacrifice my membership in an important family. I'd tell the lies required to preserve the admiration of my audience but striving to reconcile the eminence of my family and my work in the building trade left me flustered. The story I came to rely on wasn't the least bit convincing, even to myself. It was a feeble attempt to respond to a question nobody was asking, a question, I later came to realize, that troubled not a soul save myself: "Why did you leave the village?"

It was a long story, the essence of which was that my family had grown tired of me: tired of my rebellious nature and my disdain for the comfortable life. To them, disappearing off to Cairo was a form of unforgivable profligacy. When they'd finally had enough they delivered their ultimatum: do as decent folk do and live with us in the village or never darken our door again. Naturally, I chose the path of the dedicated author, or let's just say the author. When the story reached my relationship with literature I would play it down, even throw in a bit of self-mockery. Not that I passed up the opportunity to brag about my published works. I was extremely effective at directing everyone's attention to my name in print. As I undressed to begin my day's work I would carelessly toss down the newspaper or magazine and no sooner had my victim—my boss, a homeowner, any passing stranger—picked it up than I would remark, with the humility befitting an ordinary working man, "By the way, I've got a thing in there . . . ."

"Thing? What thing?" the dupe exclaims, astonished.

"I mean . . . something published . . . ."

This would usually win me an awe-struck look. Yet I always felt disconnected from the subject. The author was someone else, someone out of the ordinary. Making light of literature seemed a useful evasion, a way of excusing my scribblings and making them acceptable both to myself and to others.

That year, the year of the earthquake, the girl had failed her high school exams thereby gaining the sympathy of her mother. She was beautiful but it was a heavy, indolent beauty. Her features sagged and she had an exhausted look about her. I was much taken with the fullness of her chest, but on her it was like a stranger lost in the desert. The girl's eyes, face, and body were one thing, her chest another thing altogether.

Back at my place, inside the room in Ain Shams, I'd think about her, lingering over an image of her bending down, a movement that brought her breasts closer to my face. Down in the foundation my vision would be filled with their bounty. I would play for time and feign an inability to reach the tea tray so they could complete their orbit and all the while I'd imagine grabbing them.

I pull her to me; she falls into my embrace.

I found the idea of trapping her beneath the ground extraordinarily arousing. In the room I would revisit the scene:

The foundation dug out beneath the wall. I am inside. She bends down to pass me my tea beneath the bottom of the wall . . . . Yet whenever I got to the point where I grabbed at her, something like a battle would break out. She would squirm out of my grasp. I was fantasizing about her, but in my own fantasy she would squirm away from me, as savagely unwilling as they come.

Her parents' plan required her to visit me several times a day with lunch on a tray and two or three cups of tea, watching over me in my holes and trenches long enough to cultivate a mutual affection. She came prepared, all peaches and cream and a sash about her waist, but she never spoke, just fixed me with the gaze of one who knows what's what and, very occasionally, winked. It wasn't a wink exactly, more a spasm, the action of a person aware they are required to do something. First, she would close her right eye then, like a child who realizes it's jammed its foot in the wrong shoe, she would snap it open and resolutely close her left eye, before breaking into a smile that seemed strangely reproachful.

The business with trays of food embarrassed me. One day meat, the next chicken, and sometimes fish. Our employers never short-changed us: food, drink, and all good things. I was always embarrassed by their gifts. I never once turned them down, but I would be shy about accepting. I'd turn my face to the floor as my hand stretched out to the tray. You could consider it a desire for some kind of equilibrium: I reach out my hand and blush that it reaches out.

As for the girl, there were more important things to consider. She was hard to ignore: the only girl who was drawn to me, who gazed at me with unfeigned admiration. Yet the obviousness of things threw me. I never encouraged her or even reassured her she was on the right track. She tried and she failed. Throughout the whole ordeal I was preoccupied with another problem altogether. I was trying to perfect the role of the polite and serious young man. I would appear grave and dignified for the moment of her arrival with the food tray, the moment of a great confusion whose origins lay not in her shyness of me, or mine of her, but rather our mutual embarrassment at the whole affair.

"The foundation's finished." Thus did I address the Doctor as I handed him the final bucket. He didn't hear me. He was off in his own world. He leaned his arm against me, down in the pit, and shot up and out of the house muttering, "O Protector, O Protector . . ." only to return, panting, and stick his head back down into the trench until it was practically inside the bucket. Then he fled.

I assumed he'd had a joint on the sly. Sometimes he'd do that. I do it myself. I let the bucket drop and gripped the edge of the hole. I was expecting the marriage proposal to be waiting for me with my usual cup of tea, but there was nobody about. The house was at the end of al-Sadd Alley and when I went outside I was surprised to find the Exodus in motion. Everyone was running, just running: nothing in their minds but getting out of the alley, fleeing before a monstrous and relentlessly pursuing beast.

I went along with it half-heartedly. One foot forward, the other dragging behind. Eventually, I felt this was demeaning. Naturally I asked myself what the panic was about, but I kept running. How can you stand still while everyone else is running? Something was terrifying, no doubt about it. In the end I found what I was looking for. He was wavering between two rescue attempts: saving himself and saving the children he'd inadvertently left at home. He was still capable of volunteering a response, a response that embarrassed me further:

"Earthquake . . . an earthquake . . . . The ground underneath you is shaking . . . . These houses could fall on us any moment . . . . Are you listening? . . . Any moment now . . . ."

A Vision

And I saw, as the dreamer sees, a vast heap of sand, and I saw myself, a little bulkier than usual, hovering around it then packing it into a huge sack. In a single motion I swing the sack onto my shoulder and climb a ten-story building and fling it from me and die. I actually die. I breathe my last. But in the morning I awoke, full of energy and extraordinarily eager to get to work. I went down to the bathroom, scrubbed clean, and headed off to the café, where Mi'allim Matar hired me to take care of a load of sand in Dawaran Shubra.

I had acquired considerable expertise in unloading sand. Twice I walked around the pile and on the third revolution I had it worked out: ten meters exactly. As usual the boss deployed stalling tactics and tried to make out it was seven. I inspected the load with disbelief. It was the same pile I'd seen in my dream: the size of St. Daniel's tomb, the same yellow color, the same base, the same soft consistency, and the same slightly egg-shaped grains.

I took it all in with a single keen glance. Prophet Daniel, save me . . . . One week of pouring concrete and I flung the mixing bowl as far as it would go. Sand is much cleaner and I'm not like your run-of-the-mill laborers. This laborer business is just a temporary phase until I find my way to acceptable employment. Carrying sand is an exertion both solitary and straightforward. One plus one equals two. A struggle between a man and his strength, each sack fresh proof of your manhood, of your strength, of the fact that you're free and alone in this world.

By the time the afternoon prayer was called I had finished off the load. My body was as supple and loose as a swimmer's and it seemed to me that I could move another mountain, but then came the thought of a couple of kilos of fruit and a hot meal at Amm Ahmed's.

It was Amm Ahmed's day off from the bank and from the tea stall and of course, Hanan, his captivating daughter, was at home. I was obsessed with her. She was a tree, fruit-laden, a vine bowed down with grapes, but out of my league. How I tried! How I played the clown! So many days spent loitering around her wretched college! How often I exaggerated or, shall we say, waxed eloquent on my glorious future as a writer of note. How often I exhausted myself devising ridiculous schemes to get my stories published, and for no other reason than to draw her attention. But all to no avail. I never got so much as a word from her. Of course, we would talk about her studies, college, the weather (summer and winter), but never the one subject I was dying to broach. She would flee before my gaze, a gaze that was permanently fixed in her direction. She never showed irritation or annoyance, she just slipped away, leaving me panting and frustrated. I was, I felt, no more than a smile in her eyes. An amusing individual, perhaps a little soft in the head. I was forever trying to make her understand that I wasn't like that, that I was somebody important, creative, worthy of admiration and adoration.

Amm Ahmed's apartment consisted of a wide bed, four sofas, a bathroom, and a passageway that I'll try to describe later. Each time I visited I would rest my back against the sofa by the door and endeavor, with irreproachable decorum, to strike up a conversation. I would ask her how her studies were going, she'd reply fine, and that would be the end of it.

I would have gone over to the Earthquake Blocks where Amm Ahmed had his apartment were it not for the Doctor's surprise raids. The Doctor was a dear friend and like any man anticipating romantic conquest I saw no harm in him championing my cause before his young cousin. You might say, in fact, that his stories caused me to fall in love with her before we ever met. Nevertheless, his unexpected visits were an embarrassment, which in turn made me feel traitorous and ashamed, and so to erase my misgivings I found myself regaling her with wildly embellished accounts of his heroics. I swung the last sack over my shoulder and surrendered myself to circumstance.

Playtime

From time to time we laborers would get time off. As a general rule, and unlike the rest of the professions, manual workers have no fixed holiday. They go out looking for work and if they find it it's a working day and if they don't it's a holiday. We worked in particularly exceptional circumstances. We took advantage of the government's negligence. Fridays and official holidays were ideal for work in collapsing and dilapidated buildings but we couldn't care less. We would iron our clothes then it was out to the cinema, or Fustat Park, or the zoo. Sometimes we'd put on our tracksuits and play football at the open courts by the Suez Bridge Road. Our team was famous on the courts. We would play the young guys from nearby Heliopolis, absurdly pampered and preening, their sports kit gleaming in the afternoon sun. They intimidated us and called us hicks, and we utterly crushed them.

Other times we would go to the cinema—for the good bits, naturally: the racy scenes. I often acted the bore, proclaiming that as a means of expression, as an art, acting was suited more to women than men. A woman, it seemed to me, was an actress by nature, forced to hide that which is known to all, forced to act before a public that knows the whole truth! My voice appears to have risen. Whenever my ability for penetrating insight lets me down I bray. I'm supremely superficial, it seems, concerned only with outward appearance. As soon as I venture deeper I am thrown into confusion, even depression at times. Anyway, why be so precious? The main reason for entering the cinema was the actresses' bodies, sometimes no more than their voices.

In Fustat Park, it was a matter of stark reality: we met real girls. Its greenery was astounding, and still is, a hill of shimmering grass. In the village, verdure was all around: we planted it, we harvested it, and we ate it. Here, though, it was different. It was a luxury, something people visited on their day off. As for the girls, there were about five of them, all between junior high and the first year of high school, with round breasts and ripening bodies. We would tell ourselves they were too young for us. We were men in our late twenties and they, when all was said and done, were children. But we enjoyed playing with them. They were extremely high-spirited and came from Sayyida Zeinab. To this day I consider Sayyida Zeinab a hothouse of feminine beauty. Occasionally we'd play dumb, punting a football freighted with intent toward their chests and they would shrink away with provocative delicacy. Hala was the liveliest of all. Clowning around with her made me unbearably happy and I would try everything and anything to lure her off to another corner of the park. She'd always walk with me for a while, then pull up. Perhaps it was a suspicion of haste, of impetuosity; perhaps it was the way I looked, but something left her uncertain and fearful and made her hurry back. Even now I think of her as a lost chance. Everything seemed ready for us to make a date, to meet, to play all day in the sun.

The Doctor focused his attentions on Nourhan. Her name alone sent him into raptures and he announced to one and all that she was his and his alone. Any attempts to sidle up to her meant hostilities, if not war. Those sorts of things really were painful. If one of the guys succeeded in making Hala laugh I would be wracked with anguish and, albeit for a fleeting instant, I would seriously reconsider our friendship and contemplate the best way to scare him off. Unlike the Doctor, however, who would do so frankly and completely unapologetically, I never fought with anyone or ended a friendship. I'd swallow it. I'd act as if everything was perfectly normal. I'd stiffen, grin like a maniac, and carry on playing.

God's Work

Man, and man alone, is capable of absolutely anything. A believer, he regards every step on his way as new evidence of the truth of his faith. An infidel (a word I dislike), he sees nothing but proof of his disbelief. This thought comes to me whenever I recall the story of the time I set out to do God's work. Well, that story and others, too. There's the personal: for instance the story of my mother's pains that baffled the greatest doctors in the land, but no sooner had she planted her feet in the sands around the Prophet Daniel's tomb than she was cured and back on her feet, cantering like a pony. There's the general interest/international: like the story of Sheikh Osama Bin Laden, who, I have no doubt whatsoever, bears witness in every waking moment and incident of his life to divine miracles denied even the greatest prophets and heavenly messengers. After all, what are old cave tales such as Thaur and Hiraa when compared to the blood-curdling ambuscades and skirmishes, the deadly laser rays, from which Bin Laden escapes on a daily basis. But back to the story . . . .

I have no idea why this story returns to me with such persistence. The others I can do without—only this one remains. I always make up my mind to publish this book without it, and I always back down.

I had graduated from college and couldn't decide between living in the village and tilling the land or traveling further afield, and I . . . . No, this tale should begin from the beginning.

Until the 1970s, the only expressions of piety known to our village were the two main Muslim holy days, the festivals (most of which were clearly Christian), the call to prayer on Fridays, and the breaking of our fast at sunset during the month of Ramadan. The inhabitants had scant regard for the profession of prayer-caller, which they regarded as beneath the dignity of a Bedouin, so they made us, the children, do it for them. And truth be told, it was a daily delight. As soon as one of us performed the call to prayer we would shout for joy and scatter out of the mosque back to our families to let them know the prayer had been called, all without actually praying ourselves. I have no idea why they thought my voice was anything special, but, until Sheikh Mahmoud appeared, I became the prayer caller for Ramadan. Of course, there was no microphone. I would bellow at the top of my voice straight from the mosque's roof. But it made me happy, I enjoyed it, and before long I had developed something of a regular audience. Whenever one of my uncles showered praise on my prayer call before company I'd burst with pride. As my confidence grew I began to perfect my imitations of legendary Quran readers and prayer-callers like al-Tablawi and Abd al-Samad. The rules and skills of recitation brought me great pleasure, that is, until the learned Sheikh arrived and gave us to understand that such things were heresy, that every heresy was an error, and that all errors led to hellfire. The religiously approved, and therefore correct, call required one to produce a sustained yelp, an ugly, arid screech: Allahu Akbaarrrr, Allahu Akbaarrrr . . . .

Sheikh Mahmoud was a cousin, son of my uncle Dair Ibn Abdallah Abu Mahmoud—perhaps you remember him—and in the late seventies he passed his high school exams with flying colors (by the standards of our village, at least) and entered the Faculty of Education's English Department. When I was due to enroll in the same department, along with my cousins Sahar and Mounira and a farmer's boy called Mohamed, we went to take special lessons with the Sheikh. From the outset he was absolutely clear on one issue: only Sahar and I had any hope of passing. Mounira and the peasant needn't waste their time or his. Sahar and I diligently attended his lessons every week, and soon enough the exams came around and we were duly put to the test. Distressingly, Sahar and I failed while Mounira and Mohamed sailed through.

In the mosque, though, he was a hit. He was the vanguard of a religious awakening, if not a revolution, which quickly spread to neighboring villages. He took to delivering Friday sermons in the style of Sheikh Kishk, with the difference that in place of jibes and abuse directed at pop stars and politicians, he reserved his slings and arrows for the failings of his family and friends. The skirt chasers and cheats of whispered gossip were ruthlessly exposed at the pulpit, the Sheikh heaping down explicit threats of the torments of the Pit and searing hellfire: "So-and-so who stood by the canal to peep at the ladies shall be sent forth on the Day of Resurrection with eyes of flame and fire." Inevitably, so-and-so would turn out to be one of his relatives, and just as inevitably fights would break out. Sermon and prayers over, the battering would begin. The Sheikh won in the end. He had gathered a coterie of followers who grew out their beards and pressed the people to attend prayers and abandon their sinful ways. At first they were violent, attacking weddings, banning dancing and singing, and separating men and women. A simple little shop consisting of a mat, a stove and kettle, a couple of cartons of cigarettes, a packet of biscuits or sweets, and a solitary shisha pipe was identified by this group as the source of all sin in the village. One of my uncles had opened it to host card games and gatherings. The Brothers mounted a night raid, insulting the revelers and threatening to raze it to the ground. But the business was smothered in the cradle: the family elders gathered in the house of my uncle, the headman, and invited the Brothers over. They gave them a roasting, warned them not to step out of line, and intimated that they were headed for nothing less than a good hiding and beard plucking. In short: if you want to pray you've got the mosque and the rest is none of your business.

It was in such heightened circumstances that the Tablighi Jamaat entered the village, and in no time it had put down roots and flourished. I became a member myself. Founded by a pious Indian, it was a peaceful organization whose members promoted tolerance and treated the world around them as a capricious and impermanent vessel. It asked no more of people than to observe their prayers and follow the example of the Prophet and did not require its members—indeed, did not encourage them—to deliver sermons nor delve too deeply into the study of religious law. To listen to the group's evening message was to become a supporter, to gather your meager possessions and set out on the path of God was to be an active member. It maintained a clear and simple organizational structure. When there were three or more individuals working together, one must be elected amir, or leader, of the group, and so on up the structure: an amir for every village, an amir for each group of villages, an amir for each municipal district, and an amir for every province. The dedicated member must gather up his worldly possessions and set out on the path of God for a minimum of three days in each month, a week out of every six months, forty days in a year, and a total of four months in a lifetime. It avoids all confrontation with the authorities and absolutely forbids its members from speaking of the ills and flaws of society. It has one solitary objective: to encourage people to pray at the mosque, to relinquish their bonds to a transient world, and to set out, in turn, on the path of God. Having taken up said blanket and set out, they make you deliver the group's evening message. Directly after the prayers they would say to you, "Stand, Sheikh, and God will inspire you . . . ." At which point you wouldn't recognize the alphabet if it introduced itself. But it's true, He does inspire you. He inspired me, and there I was, preaching to people, exhorting them with zeal and conviction to hold fast to God and turn their backs on a treacherous world.

Its most dedicated members possess a rotundity and calm that comes from long hours spent sleeping in mosques and an ease of mind borne of the certain belief that all suffering is fate. In our village the group's message was spread by my cousin, a man for whom I continue to harbor the utmost respect and admiration. He was one of those men who had left their worldly lives behind them and declared: I belong to God. His life was given entirely to prayer and exalting the word of God. In the 1990s he did God's work in Sudan, Indonesia, Pakistan, and Afghanistan and he was the one who persuaded me to do likewise. Three days is nothing in a man's lifetime, as he put it, and I was too ashamed to refuse outright. I tried claiming that I smoked, but he just told me to smoke all I liked. God's work didn't stop you smoking. A group of youths from the village went to stay in a neighboring village for three days, and there we split into two teams: an external team that went from house to house calling on people to pray in the mosque and an internal team that sat in the mosque reciting the names of God and making supplications to the Almighty to grant success to the Brothers in the external team. All day the smells of cooking would fill the mosque and the food itself was heavenly. We'd descend on it like climbers falling off a mountain. It was the most comfortable three days of my life. It is a great solace to lie down at night, your eyelids drooping, knowing that all that befalls you, good or ill, is fate. We were truly at peace. I gained relief from those feelings of responsibility and guilt that haunted me then, and haunt me now, and will continue to do so for the rest of my days.

The Pricking of My Conscience

I woke at six, as usual. It was freezing; icy. It was Ramadan at the time and I just couldn't be bothered. I still had to get up, go down to the bathroom, squeeze onto a bus. Then what? Hanging around at the café. I might get work, and then again, I might not. I pulled the blanket tighter and closed my eyes. I was almost asleep again when my conscience perked up: "So why are you here, then? Isn't it time to work? Fine, forget work for the moment. What about money? Got any with you?"

Panicking, I jumped to my feet and sprinted down to the bathroom. I showered, dressed, and shot off to Shubra.

I was the only one from the village there. It was a pleasant little café and I said to myself there's work today if you're lucky. There were four guys from Beni Suef and myself. At eight Mi'allim Matar walked in: a man of regular habits, except when it came to paying wages. He smoked his usual shisha, Ramadan or no, and took two guys for a demolition job in the Sheikh Ramadan apartments. Matar left and a skimmer arrived and took someone to mix the plaster. Then a private client walked in and took the last of them to lug furniture downstairs and I was left alone, waiting. "What's the time?" I asked Salim. "Nine thirty," he replied, in a voice that made it clear there was no point in waiting further.

That's life. The market rises and falls. The winners win and the losers lose.

I began adjusting my plan for the day: in place of a day spent working I thought of ways to waste it. Normally, I'd go back to the room in Ain Shams and pass the hours reading, masturbating, sleeping, and spying on the neighbors (after the fast was over for the day, of course). I considered taking a little trip to go and see the Doctor but couldn't make up my mind if that constituted appropriate behavior during the blessed month. I concluded that it was because in all probability the actress wouldn't come out during the day, and I could sleep until sunset, break my fast with the Doctor, then return to Ain Shams.

Every time we met he would invite me to come and take a look at the actress. He'd told me that she preferred him to the other workers in the building and had given him the task of bringing her her fan letters. She would usually only open colored or decorated envelopes. She would gaze at each opened letter in disgust and throw it at the Doctor, carrying on until there were none left. "Take this trash away," she'd say, and he'd pick them up and go downstairs. He told me that she had befriended a mysterious Saudi lady. Now and again I would visit the Doctor, racy scenes from her films flickering through my mind, and sit on the bench outside watching him work and waiting for her to appear. When she did appear, however, I'd make it as clear as I could that she meant less than nothing to me. I'd raise my gaze to the heavens and let her pass by as though she were no more than air. Once she came up to me and, with the calm that comes before a storm, asked, "Who are you? A relative of that idiot over there?" I instantly resolved to disavow all connection with that idiot over there, but she was already all over me:

"Stand up straight when you talk to me!"

I panicked. Sweat coated me.

"Say something . . . . Have you lost your voice?"

To be honest, I had. Things were going wrong, I felt. There was no call for proud defiance: she could get me into a lot of trouble. The Doctor saved me. He came running over, waving toward the building's basement, and said that I was a customer and that I'd be on my way as soon as my car was brought up from the garage.

At the Sheikh Ramadan bus stop I took a bus for Ramses, where I changed for Heliopolis. I got off opposite the Doctor's building: ten floors over a basement and the Doctor right outside. He was wearing jeans and a tight shirt stretched at the belly and polishing cars with great energy and devotion. As he saw me he gave a shout and we fell on each other, all kisses and hugs.

I sat for a bit on the bench outside. I asked if he wouldn't mind if I slept in his room and to leave me be until we broke fast. I went in and fell asleep. Fast asleep. I dreamt of a beautiful woman in my arms. I felt her up from top to bottom and was about to start doing to her what one does in dreams when it became obvious that she was real. A real body, soft and smooth as dough. I scrambled back in fright only to find the Doctor looming over the bed.

"What's going on?" I asked.

"It's fine, just not right now, okay? They're fasting. After we've broken our fast, God willing."

I suddenly became aware of a second girl sprawled in a maximally provocative position on a nearby bed. I'd heard bits and pieces here and there about what went on in the building, but I'd never imagined it was quite so blatant. Actually, I was frightened. I reviewed the full range of divine and mortal punishment. Until that point I had lived more or less in my imagination: two experiences, maybe more, that there's no point in dwelling on here. We waited until the breaking of fast, which gave me a chance to regroup and absorb the situation. Then it happened, an incident that gave me no peace for a long time afterward and still disturbs my sleep to this day. It happened so simply, with such ease and gentle care, that I can still savor its taste on my lips. We went to a wooden bed in the basement. I quickly lost my nerve, of course, but she was understanding. "Calm down," she told me, "Take your time . . ." and showered me with such a sweet and joyous tenderness as would have brought a corpse to life.

Standing on Solid Ground

The Doctor had a relationship with a woman from the village. It would die down and flare up, but it would be on his mind constantly. After he'd had a couple of joints and his mind was bright he'd talk of nothing else. It was a truly peculiar relationship. She couldn't tell what the Doctor wanted from her. Hanan, it was: his cousin's wife. He tried to sleep with her and she tried to sleep with him, and that was it. He did her in his dreams and for years now had considered trying her out for real. She, too, wanted to try with him, and him in particular. She had already slept with every man of her acquaintance who had shown the slightest inclination: her husband's two younger brothers, her colleague at work, two young men from our family, one of my uncles, and two or three chance encounters. Only the Doctor remained. Let it not be said she didn't make an effort. She laid the groundwork and set up trysts that her husband would never suspect. Her husband wasn't bothered. He didn't want to know, if you see what I mean. He'd excuse himself and leave them alone for hours, pulling up the blanket and going off to sleep halfway through the evening. But at some point the Doctor would always give up. The moment she was ready for action and worked up he would take his leave and she'd see him off with a look of contempt that troubled him not the least. He'd make a joke of her anger. I used to feel that he was punishing her, but also that he was afraid of her. He went with others, girls and women, in the village and the building where he worked. The story of him sleeping with his neighbor with the door wide open was famous in our village and further afield. But she was something else. Hanan was different. Hanan was no pushover: young and beautiful and strong and shameless. He'd reach out to her in his mind. He'd close his eyes and make her kneel. But reality and imagination are very different things.

She was from a family of Gypsies who lived in a nearby village. She had studied with us at junior high, where she won a certain notoriety for the size of her breasts. They weren't immense or anything, just not the size you tend to get on little girls in junior high. She was poor. Her clothes were filthy and she sat on the bench at the back of the class, as though embarrassed by the size of her chest.

The Doctor studied with her for two years, the first two years, and like her, he sat in the back row. He'd heard that she had been through nursing college but didn't start paying attention properly until she married his cousin. She became something else altogether: a woman, composed and sexy and capable of stirring the most violent emotions. The Doctor followed her progress keenly, picking up bits of news and gossip in the village, in Shubra, and anywhere else he could. He was always the first to hear about each and every man she slept with. One of the greatest regrets of his life was the day of the trench. He was at his cousin's house digging a trench to lay the plumbing. In our village the newer houses are equipped with more or less modern bathroom facilities and sewage pipes, and the Doctor was usually the one who would get these jobs: construction, plastering, or installing the plumbing.

It's rocky ground where we live. She waited for him to dig down nice and deep and began to flirt outrageously. She wouldn't come near him until he was down in the trench. She'd sit on the edge and leave her legs to dangle down, right over him, wearing her robe and nothing else. The Doctor, positioned beneath her, almost had a seizure. He sprang out of the trench.

"I'm going to go crazy."

"You've gone crazy?"

"Just once, I'm begging you, just once."

"Not today. Tomorrow I'll wait for you. If you're late that's your choice."

So he left. The Doctor left, though the day was yet young and he should have been working in the trench, preferring to give himself plenty of time to prepare. He drew on his experience at the pharmacy, prescribing a pill that delays, if not prevents, ejaculation, and rolled himself a couple of respectably sized joints. Next day, he grabs his chisel and flies over to his cousin's trench. She meets him at the door, he enters, becomes confused, and finds himself descending into the trench and digging away like a trooper.

Amm Ahmed

Amm Ahmed had two apartments in the Earthquake Blocks in west Ain Shams: one on the top floor, one on the ground floor with a small garden overflowing with plants of every kind. He's originally from our part of the world, the Doctor's uncle. He came to Cairo in the seventies and started out as a laborer until he made a success of working as an office boy in the headquarters of Banque Misr, supplementing his income with a tea stall on Mansour Street. He was living in Boulaq and after the earthquake he patiently endured queues at government offices until he was housed in the Ain Shams housing projects named, in reference to its residents and their recent history, the Earthquake Blocks. At first it was just the one apartment—Apartment 1, Block 5—and Amm Ahmed was in a quandary. "The boy will marry and live with me in the apartment, but what about the girl?" A cooperative here, a cooperative there, a couple of extra cups at the tea stall, and he'd solved the problem. He bought a flat on the top floor and everyone, even the neighbors, could see that the son would marry and stay on the ground floor and the daughter would live in the new flat. Amm Ahmed decided that he had done what was asked of him in this life. He relaxed, grew fat, and began to move around as if lord and master of the building, one moment going upstairs to the top floor apartment and the girl, the next coming downstairs to stay with his son. Emboldened by possession of the two apartments, he went and put his hands on government property, knocking down the wall on his ground floor balcony and incorporating a piece of land that he dug up and turned over until he had transformed it into a flourishing little garden. His life was progressing in a calm and orderly fashion, the only cloud on the horizon being his wife. She was short, mean, and from Beni Suef, a little troublemaker addicted to nagging, grudges, and double-dealing. She would constantly feign some illness or other and generally force him to put up with more than he could bear.

I loved his company and his conversation and was forever visiting him at home or at the tea stall. At first I thought I was drawn there by his daughter, but I came to realize that it was him I loved. He was a generous man, a man who loved people, and he treated me like a son, confiding his deepest secrets and asking my advice on everything. I would follow his news with the devotion and dedication usually accorded a father or older brother. I would be delighted whenever he asked for my help with anything, but he rarely did so. He gave only: food and drink and eyes that danced for joy to see me. To me his life seemed as full of incident as a soap opera on TV. And while it certainly seemed regular as clockwork—rising at six every day and donning his blue suit, off to work at the bank until two in the afternoon and then to the tea stall where he'd pass the evening, and finally returning home at two in the morning, a copy of *al-Akhbar* folded beneath his arm—nothing stays the same for long. By some happy chance it fell to me to announce the tidings of his wife's death. She was an oppressive presence. She resented our visits and almost put us off coming to see him altogether. She was always pretending to be sick, and I used to bitch about her to the Doctor—and Amm Ahmed himself—and remark that she was in danger of fulfilling the saying of the Prophet: "Feign not illness lest you fall ill and die." Sure enough, while I was working up in Shubra, the prophecy came to pass and she dropped dead. A few months after that, the two children finally accepted the idea that the living are more important than the dead and got married, the girl to her cousin and the boy to one of the neighbors' daughters. For a while Amm Ahmed divided his time between them: a couple of days with the girl, a couple with the boy, and Friday in the garden planting and weeding. But then, as is ever the case with Man, the problems started: resentment, jealousy, ill will, and rising tempers. Amm Ahmed craved the simple life once more. What to do? He was on the verge of retirement. I thought he would give up, or at best go off to live on his own far from the troubles at home, but he went and surprised us all with a bride, a lusty young girl from Beni Suef. He set a date with the Doctor and me, and we brought a couple of day laborers with us and went to the garden where we built him a room hooked up to the water and electricity. Amm Ahmed excused himself and traveled down to Beni Suef. He returned a mere two days later with his young bride and, in his new room, we put on a wedding to remember.

A Fleeting Visit

The Doctor visited Daniel in prison. Daniel is a relative, a neighbor, and a good friend. He's the one who got us the room in Ain Shams and it was only proper that we pay him a visit to see how he was doing. They chewed over the difference between jail time and life on the outside and the Doctor almost asked him whether you could get time off for good behavior in cases of embezzlement and bribery. They agreed that it was only a matter of days and they'd end soon enough, and the Doctor took some money to pass on to his wife—our contemporary, our neighbor, and the object of many fantasies in the village, in Ain Shams, and in the bathroom—and folded it into his pocket. He strolled over to the east side of the village and rapped on a door. In our village doors are never locked, day or night, but this particular door was. She opened up and he said that he'd come straight from prison to see her and that her man was fine, wished her a good morning, and in he went.

The house, as is usually the case in our village (located as it is in the middle of the desert), was spacious and they both decided to continue their conversation in the inner room. They followed a little flock of ducks waddling boisterously into the interior. Suddenly and simultaneously they became aware of the sensitivity of their situation, of gossip, and of the Bedouin and what they might do. They were embarrassed. She opened the door to the house, propped it open with a stone, and said, "That's better."

She was about twenty-six or -seven and looked the same as she does now: short, pale, and plump. She sat down on the mat and shuffled toward him, letting her dress slip from her calves. I have no idea whether this happened by accident or design, or whether it merely pleased the Doctor to believe he saw it, but it struck right at his most vulnerable spot. This was something that never failed to fire both my imagination and that of an entire generation. Each one of the girls we grew up with was known for something. With her, it was the calves. The sight of her rubbing them smooth for hours by the banks of the canal was a shining high point in our memories. It was, I would venture to say, the first notable sight, the first burning ember, in the lives of many young men in our village. If I weren't so worried about what people might say, I'd tell you that the scene stays with me even now. Even as I write, I can see myself seducing her away from the bank . . . but that's another matter.

Back to the point . . . the Doctor sat facing her, every torrid scene in his imagination unfolding before his mind's eye, and handed her the cash. "Look sharp!" he told himself, "She's right there for the taking." They went to the door. Open and resting against a stone, it was a comfort to the neighbors and to the two of them alike. How could anyone sleep with a girl with the door wide open?

The Laborer

I heard that they were traveling to Cairo to work as laborers. I asked them: what's this laborer thing? Naturally, I didn't expect that they were working as pilots. I knew that they were workmen and that they carried sacks around. An uncle of mine told his son, "Take yourself off to Cairo and get some muck on your clothes instead of sitting around here." But the word laborer fascinated me. Why laborer? 'Working as a laborer.' Why did it refer to the toughest and most exhausting work? But when I made the journey myself and started work I saw that it was entirely appropriate, scrupulously exact. It is the primal act, immutable and timeless: lifting something from one place to another.

I'd taken my middle school certificate, got the results I needed, and was all set for high school. I wanted a bike, dreamt of it; something to mess around on and a way to get to school. I went with a group: the Doctor and three or four guys from the village. I was ready for work. I was ready from the moment I left the house. I could have made the journey in a shirt and trousers—the Doctor did—but I wore instead a striped Bedouin gallabiya. We got off at Ahmed Hilmi and caught a bus to Shubra. It was crowded and I stood behind another passenger. Maybe because I was still wet behind the ears, or perhaps because it never rains but it pours, I kept falling against him and he appeared to misread the situation. Well, really, he turned out to be right, but anyway: he gave me a consummately skillful and unexpected bump with his buttocks that caused me to sustain an erection. I shuffled closer and pressed into him. I became thoroughly preoccupied, but when my interest was at its height he turned to me and said, "Take it easy. Don't get so worked up," and I shriveled away. Practically dead from shame, I got straight off the bus and luckily it turned out to be my stop.

We were met by Mi'allim Matar, who to my surprise was an old man, in his sixties perhaps, and wearing a suit. He hired us to carry sand and dirt down from the roof of a collapsing building in Dawaran Shubra. It was a mountain of rubble and rubbish and we were a while getting it down, two whole weeks, but it was the best time working in Shubra I ever had. I got fifty pounds, went back to the Fayoum, bought a bike, and entered my village riding upon it.

A Reception Fit for a General

I don't know why I joined the demonstration. I don't know why I didn't run for it the first chance I got. I could have: I got close to the wall and thought of making a break for it. The students were fleeing all around me, singly and in groups, and even the soldier told me to do it: "Jump up and run," he said, "before they catch you." I'm a naturally submissive type, instinctively terrified of the police and security forces, and by rights I should've run, I should've flown like a bird. But I was ashamed, embarrassed to hop up onto the wall like that and take off, so I turned back. If only I hadn't.

It was the end of the first term and I was drifting. I had failed to implement the plan to retake my high school exams and improve my score, nor was I attending college regularly. That's a failing of mine, unfortunately: I'm never content with my lot, or indeed, with my life. But then I never did anything to change it. Occasionally I'd travel up to Cairo, work a week or two and return, and I only went to college to leer at the girls and stay up late with friends. The morning of the demonstration I had turned up at the college at about ten and noticed that it was surrounded by security forces. I wasn't bothered. Recently, the security forces had taken to surrounding everything. In the courtyard outside I saw a knot of Brothers gathered, but that didn't bother me either. Recently, the Brothers had taken to gathering in self-important circles and marching around. I climbed to the third floor. People were murmuring that the Brothers were going to stage a demonstration to protest against the crosses that unknown elements were spray-painting on the Sisters' clothes, or to demand the release of two of their leaders incarcerated in Tora Prison. I don't remember exactly. I went down to take a look. A vast crowd was assembled beneath the dean's window and chanting as one in a voice like thunder. Again, I don't know why, but a strange intoxication took hold of me and I began chanting with them, "Coward! Agent of the Americans!" Yes: intoxication, mixed with something like joy and disdain, and I gazed out at the security forces ringing the campus with a real sense of superiority and contempt.

The dean appeared at his window and demanded that the students disperse and return to their studies or he would ask the police to enter the college. The devastating response came in the form of a chair hurled by a Sister standing directly beside me. And then (may you be spared such sights) the revolution broke out, a genuine revolution directed against the furniture. Students—Brothers and non-Brothers alike—laid waste to the college, to the classrooms and despised lecture halls, in a barbaric frenzy of destruction. The legions of the law sealed off the campus from all directions and began issuing warnings. The Brothers responded with bricks; volleys of red brick. Naturally, I didn't take part in this. The whole while I remained somewhat confused and disoriented. I would run for a bit, then stop, and then, for no clear reason, sit down. But what a sense of pride I had, a real sense of pride, to see them bombard the security troops with bricks. There was this stack of red bricks in the courtyard, which they had relocated in its entirety onto the heads of the police. The cops reacted by firing bombs; little bombs that the Brothers would snatch up and throw back. They gave off this awful smoke. My eyes caught fire. I stumbled up to the bathroom on the second floor. I subsequently learned that the correct treatment involves an onion and not water, which only makes it worse. I crashed out into the corridor screaming, where it was my great misfortune to run into Khalil, the dean's detestable lackey. He loathed me. I was forever making fun of him and had succeeded in turning him into something of a joke on campus. Though I could barely see a thing through the sheets of tears and the dense smoke, his bald spot and diminutive stature gave him away. I would have to throw myself on his mercy. I embraced him violently and, despite his small size, managed to insert myself beneath his armpit.

"Save me, Mr. Khalil," I said with all the wretchedness and humility I could muster. "Come here, little one," he said, "don't be frightened," but in the villainous tone of the scumbag who sees his chance. When we reached the top of the stairs he gave savage expression to his lack of scruples . . . and pushed.

At the college gate an armored host of Central Security troops waited, rank upon rank, sufficient to blot out the sun. Beefy soldiers marched in circles, stamping their feet, and grunting en masse *(Hurgh!)* while a gang of officers and soldiers was busy wiping the floor with a student I knew. Outside, only a short distance away and ready to welcome the fallen and the detained, the central security forces truck stood like a life jacket just out of reach. How I wished I could just close my eyes and open them again to find myself inside. How I wished, too, for the ground to split open and swallow me up. Suddenly, I noticed this officer nearby sort of flip into the air (I swear to God) and come flying at me legs-first like a pair of tongs. I screamed, practically fell over backward, and said, "I surrender. I'm handing myself in." Words uttered in despair, commending myself to God's tender mercy . . . and then the miracle happened. I heard a voice give the order, "Leave him!" The officers and soldiers fell into two parallel, unwavering lines, and I was left to walk between them, safe and sound, for all the world like some general, until I reached the truck and climbed in.

A Letter

My dear brother,

Greetings and affection. I hope that you are well and that my aunt and Ahmed and Zeinab and Somaya and their children are all as well as can be.

Give my love to Aunt Miriam and her children and to Uncle Mukhtar's family. Tell them that I sent him a letter and he never replied and I don't why. Was the address wrong or is he busy? Give my love to Ayman and Khalid and Shihab.

Anyway . . . .

Let me remind you that we're brothers and there are no unpaid checks or IOUs between us. Also, let me just say that if I had any money I would never hold it back from you, ever.

As for the work visa, it should cost about 4,000 Egyptian pounds. The Bahraini guy will take the money in exchange for the visa. He will take it before he does anything. Also, it's a risk because you might take a month or two months or three months to get work, so it's the sort of thing that depends on God's blessing and your luck. You should know as well that I've only got a thousand and a half with me here, but I've been asked to pay a down payment of 3,500 pounds within five months of travel, so in other words I'm really tight for cash and I don't have a penny extra, may God be with me.

I spoke to the owner of the travel agency about you and he said he will see if he's got anything for you. If he manages to get you a contract I will let you know what he needs from you. If we are lucky you can spend the money at home and I will give what I've got to the Bahraini. If he wants more then I will get you to bring it with you from Egypt.

I hope you realize that I am not getting anything out of this for myself. Actually, I'm making friends with this guy and spending money on him so that I can get some work for one of you. To date this has cost me about 250 Egyptian pounds and so long as I have just one pound for myself I won't ask you to pay it back until you are out here with me.

The visa lasts for two years. It's a work visa and the salaries are between 80 and 100 dinars. Monthly expenditure for one person is about 52 dinars.

A Film

I keep thinking of writing a film about the time the Doctor spent in the actress's building. While we were working up in Shubra my imagination would run away with me: the film was finished and it had rocked the world. I still see it as a good way of improving my prospects. Whenever money gets tight I turn to my copy of *Learn to Write a Film Script* and begin preparing for my masterwork.

The Doctor returned from his stint as a driver's mate a wreck, skin on bone, lines of cement creasing his face. But he didn't come back to Shubra. It seemed he'd made up his mind to give up working as a laborer and started distributing videotapes. He wore an all-denim outfit and spent months traipsing around the video stores. He took me along for a bit. He said it's clean work and the money's guaranteed, not like grubbing about in the building trade, but we found neither money nor cleanliness, just a group of deeply unpleasant and frigid people. The whole trade—the agents, the kids in the stores, even the customers—it was like they were queers. No, not queers exactly: unmanly. All you'd get from them was a nasty smile, whether mocking or pitying it was hard to tell. We spent months earnestly distributing videos to the stores in Shubra and the surrounding areas and in the end they cheated us.

The Doctor worked for a while in a garage, then a bakery, and then a fabric shop, but he could never concentrate on the task at hand. The whole time he was dreaming of being a doorman. He'd describe it as a fitting end for someone like himself: you sit on your bench, you take your money, and you watch the people coming and going. He took the whole thing very seriously, as usual. He did his research and narrowed it down to one particular building—the actress's building in Heliopolis—sacrificing his life savings of two hundred pounds for the chance to work there.

He worked as an assistant to Abdu. Abdu was the official doorman, a dark-skinned, idle, shifty Nubian who couldn't keep his mouth shut. Beneath the large building was a basement level containing a garage and seven rooms constructed out of chipboard partitions. The room where the drivers slept had a working door and lock but the rest were just divided off from the garage with curtains and set aside for the business. By day it was girls in black gallabiyas and scarves, by night it was little madams in the latest outfits. The customers were of two types. The headscarves and gallabiyas got all the drivers, doormen, and domestics in the neighborhood and the fashionable ones (or "the little hotties" as the Doctor would refer to them in conversation with their wealthy clients) tended to work outside. A bey would pull up in his car, grab a girl, and shoot off. I hope you don't think that this was prostitution. It was purely altruistic. Honest. A humanitarian service provided by Abdu the doorman for free, or at least for considerably less than he deserved. I don't know quite how to put it, but the man genuinely loved what he was doing. He was good at it. He'd extend the invitation to people he had only just met. It gave him a peculiar pleasure to perch on his bench in front of the building with a client riding one of the girls inside.

Naturally, the Doctor knew all about it. Perhaps it was the reason he thought of the building in the first place; however, the moment he found himself caught up in the middle of it, he took fright. The terrifying specters of the law, village tradition, Wrong and Right, and searing hellfire loomed up before him. He decided to keep to himself (his motto: "Morning, sunshine! You mind your business and I'll mind mine"), throwing himself body and soul into his work. He would sweep the staircase and the entrance, wash his share of the cars, run errands for the residents, then take himself off to one side. When the business started up he'd leave the place altogether.

His resistance didn't last long. The fact that the operation was clearly philanthropic in nature reassured and emboldened him. For a while after that he allowed his actions to be directed by the well-known philosophical premise that "that's one thing and this is quite another," and would finish his business with a girl as quickly as he could in order to make the mosque on time. Before long he'd gotten to know the drivers and became one of the gang.

There were about seven of them. Every Thursday they held a party with the hotties in the room of the senior driver, Alaa, private chauffeur to the bashmuhandis. Drinking and dancing and group sex. The Doctor had a ball. He would tell these stories, like the one about the minx who'd latch onto a guy like a pair of pincers and wouldn't let go until he was as lifeless as a corpse, or the night one of the girls threw herself naked into his arms for no better reason than to extinguish the fire of her envy, which was being fanned by another girl who lay moaning beneath a driver on the bed opposite. But he could never fully relax around them. He was uneasy, haunted by doubt and fear and overwhelming guilt. He was forever expecting them to do something to him while he was drunk, or that they'd be raided by the cops and the others would pin it on him. He didn't know what to do: he was in no position to give up the job, but neither could he cope with its attendant dangers. His train of thought led him to cover his own back; to take measures to ensure he could prove that he had nothing to do with the whole affair. I have no idea whether it was excessive caution or simply a lust for revenge that led him to record them: one and a half hours of intoxication, debauchery, and the sort of loose talk about the actress, her friend, and their upper-crust visitors that leads straight to a jail cell.

I wish the Doctor had kept that tape. At the very least it would have set him apart from the rest if the shit ever did hit the fan, and anyway, having it around would be a pleasure in itself.

A Traitor and an Informer

The central security truck was as packed as a public bus. Fifty students hale and hearty, a disabled student, and a student who turned out to be the son of a police officer and got out before we started to move. As I got in I saw a student I recognized. We'd never had much to do with each other but the moment we saw each other we shrieked and embraced in an ecstasy of relief. Staggering about, we both spoke simultaneously, "Did you see? Did you see what happened?" then burst into an uncontrollable torrent of giggles. I tried to pull myself together, reminding myself of the slaps and kicks to come, but it was no good. We were past caring, every one of us, and then it was all playful punches and slaps on shoulders, buttocks, and the backs of our necks. Even the soldiers were laughing. They took us from the college to the Beni Suef Directorate of State Security, and the entire journey was spent doubled up with laughter. Had you seen us in our security truck you would've thought we were on a school trip or off to a wedding.

They ordered us to place our hands on our heads and we stepped down into the tender care of the Beni Suef State Security. They stood in two lines, commanded us to sit, and blindfolded us.

We were led off, two by two, to meet some doubtlessly dangerous individual. From time to time I would hear shrieks and moans and by the time they pulled me up I was petrified. With each step forward my death drew closer. To be dragged around blindfolded in a place like the Beni Suef State Security headquarters is a terrifying thing. We walked what seemed a fair distance. I was later told it was no more than a hundred meters but I'd bet good money that it was at least a kilometer. The trick is blind obedience: convince the person pulling you along that he has some abject and piteous wretch on his hands. Upstairs, downstairs, along passages, and through corridors, until I became aware that we had, at last, come into the presence of others. I pictured myself standing before them blindfolded. I thought: these must be individuals so menacing and shadowy that we have to be blindfolded so we can't see them. The sounds of breathing and murmuring drew suddenly closer. My hands were still on my head and I flinched down in fright but was a little encouraged by a sudden, collective guffaw.

"Don't be frightened," one of them said and proceeded to recite, in the calm voice of a soldier listing name and rank, "From the Fayoum, Itsa Daniel municipality, father deceased, supported by his mother along with four other siblings, two sons and two daughters, source of income a single feddan of land left by his father." With noticeable gentleness he inquired, "Why did you participate in the demonstration, Hamdi?"

"I swear to God I didn't participate, I was standing in the . . . ."

He cut me off.

"No need to swear by God, Hamdi, we know everything. Now then, what do you think of the President of the Republic?"

I said, "I swear I don't know him," almost immediately, then started backtracking, "I mean . . . I mean . . . ."

I got stuck on "I mean . . . ."

"It's okay," he said. "Now, what is it that you do know about him?"

"Who, sir?" I said.

"The President."

"I don't know anything," I replied. "Nothing. I see him on TV and in the papers and that's it." I was on the verge of wishing the President a long life and good health, but thought he might misunderstand me.

"Right. What do you think of His Excellency the Minister of the Interior?"

"That he's the Minister of the Interior."

"You are accused of illegal assembly, the destruction of public property, and conspiracy to overthrow the ruling regime."

I kept up my protestations that I had nothing to do with it, that I was just standing around at the college. He turned to my fellow inmate. His answers put me to shame. They were so unwavering and courageous that the officer himself was intimidated and would only ask him two questions, to which he received a single response.

"What is your opinion of the President?"

"A coward and an informer. Fighting and killing him is lawful for every Muslim."

"What is your opinion of His Excellency the Minister of the Interior?"

"The same. A coward and an informer and the leader of a bunch of thugs. The shedding of his blood is sanctioned by divine law."

Out we went. I thanked God that I could leave walking on my own two feet. They led us blindfolded back to the detention cells where the Brothers were chanting and the sound of their voices shook the State Security Directorate and the town of Beni Suef itself. Actually, I was in awe of them, but I concentrated on saying my prayers. I'd heard one of them say, "The Prophet, may the peace and prayers of God be upon him, once said that whoever repeated *God, deliver me from harm and the wiles of the deceitful, for Thou art the All-Hearing and All-Knowing* three times would be protected from all evil by day and by night." I said it ten times, tens of times. I was searching for an exit: a way out of the mess I'd gotten myself into.

I had a relative who was an army officer, later martyred by the bullets of the Palestinian resistance in Rafah in the seventies. In those days he was working for the quartermaster corps in Beni Suef, so I asked for him through one of the soldiers and he turned up. It would have been better if he hadn't. Instead of consoling me or offering to help he just terrified me even more. The instant he caught sight of me he let fly: "Why are you in here? What got you locked up with these people? What's your problem?" I stopped him there. "I've got enough questions to deal with," I said. "I've got questions coming out of my ears. If you're going to do something then do it, if you can't, goodbye." He muttered to himself and stormed out. The next time I saw him was inside the Beni Suef General Prison.

A Plot of Land

Everybody knows where to find the laborers. Their markets are on top of bridges or at the edge of public squares. But we were too proud to sit out in the sun. Our spot was Salim's café at the beginning of Muniyat al-Seirig Street in the direction of Sheikh Ramadan. I liked it because of Salim. He wasn't the owner, though he acted the part, and he endeared himself to me because he made it clear he thought manual labor was beneath us. "A great bunch of guys," he'd call us. "Not the sort that should be scrabbling around in construction."

Sitting at the café meant no guarantees. Your chances of finding work were roughly equal to your chances of going home and spending the day in bed back in your room. When Matar was going through one of his inactive patches we would take work with anyone, anywhere. Once, I went with an individual who said he was a contractor and we agreed that I'd dig the foundations for a building in Haram. He took me out there in his car and we inspected the site: a plot of land surrounded by a wall. "Work hard," he said. "A foundation trench is twenty pounds. Payment at the end of the day." He got into his car and departed. I worked hard. I dug out two trenches. The end of the day arrived and he didn't come. He must have been held up for some reason. The next day I returned, purely to give him a piece of my mind and take my money for the foundations, yet the moment I crossed into the enclosure I decided that I might as well spend my time digging a trench. When he came I'd ask for sixty rather than forty. By the third day I'd given up. I was digging for nothing. Even so, I couldn't let go of the idea that my trenches were a strategic reserve. For months afterward, whenever the café let me down, I would return to the foundations with hopes of receiving my just reward, but I never saw a soul.

Military Prison

At night they transferred us to a place nearby that we were told was the military prison. It felt like a chamber beneath the sea, beneath the eternal Nile, a long, dark basement, its interior coated—or rather sprayed—in cement from top to bottom. At one end stood a lavatory that leaked in every direction. When we arrived the place was full of bunk beds. They made us stand outside for ages while they carried them out. They brushed and scrubbed the room clean and we entered. A soldier handed me a sheet of newspaper (*al-Wafd*, I think). I spread it out on the ground and slept. To be precise, I jerked off quickly so that I'd sleep better . . . and so I did. I dreamt I was being tortured.

I awoke to find that I was being tortured. At first I thought I must still be asleep, so I lay still and waited. I was undoubtedly being tortured: a painful jabbing or stabbing sensation in my side. Thus it begins, I told myself, scrambled to my feet in fright, and got ready to run, only to find myself staring into a friendly smile, which said, "Morning prayers, Brother." I wanted to throttle him. Instead I dusted myself down, performed the ritual ablutions, and we all prayed together and went back to sleep. I was woken by a patch of sunlight streaming in through the small hatch, around which we would crowd each morning. A day passed, and a second, and a third, and things never changed. At night we would carpet the basement with newspaper and sleep, and during the day we would jostle around the hatch. Naturally, rumors were rife and continually evolving. Some said we were being detained until the revolution (launched by the residents of Beni Suef when they heard of our arrest) had petered out and we would all be free soon enough. Some said news of the affair had spread beyond Beni Suef, that the BBC had mentioned us by name in a radio broadcast, and that the affair was now in the hands of the highest authorities in the land. We'd be transferred to Tora Prison, or perhaps the oases. Whenever we asked them when we would be released they said, "Tomorrow."

"Tomorrow," they'd tell us, always "Tomorrow," and I came to hate the word. It would have been easier if they had said in a year, in ten years even, because then I would've known my fate and could relax.

One tomorrow, just before dawn, they took us all to the state security prosecutor. We were ushered into his office and found him to be a young man, and openly sympathetic. "Don't worry," he told us, "We've all done it," and offered us cigarettes, tea, and biscuits. I had a smoke and became so deeply unwound that I nodded off in the chair.

The interrogation began.

"You are charged with illegal assembly with more than five other individuals, the destruction of public property, and conspiracy to overthrow the ruling regime."

Before I had a chance to reply he turned to his assistant and dictated, "It never happened." He smiled at me and said, "You going to tell me how to do my job? Going to teach me to be a lawyer?"

He asked his questions and supplied the answers that would guarantee my immediate release. They even apologized to me.

By noon they were loading us back onto trucks that left Beni Suef heading north. People in the street were pointing at us and some of them called out, "Allahu Akbar." It seemed for an instant that the Tora Prison rumor had been spot on, but then the trucks turned off the road and entered the Beni Suef General Prison. We were met by the governor, an affable young man with an upturned mustache who calmed our fears and was generally reassuring. He said that we were guests here, that we would be released eventually, and that we were being detained to allow the town's inhabitants to settle down. He would not order our heads to be shaved and we would keep our own clothes. However, he warned us about the prisoners, emphasizing the length of time they had been subject to certain deprivations. They were all murderers and lifers. The shortest sentences in the place were ten to fifteen years.

"Naturally, a man in such a position will yearn for a breath of fresh air, and we won't be held responsible. If you choose not to keep your eyes open that's your lookout."

We were dismissed.

The prison building was in the shape of a long rectangle, three or four floors high, each floor connected to the next by iron staircases with banisters. The cells were arranged in two rows facing each other and opened onto a long, narrow corridor that for the duration of our exercise breaks was transformed into a marketplace. It was a proper emporium. Everything was available, from seeds and peanuts to weed and hashish.

We were assigned two cells on the third floor, home to murderers and thieves and the like, and handed a couple of blankets each. I can't tell you how relieved I was when I heard that the bearded students would go to one cell and the beardless to the other.

The prisoners mobbed us the moment we walked into the cell. It was a welcome fit for heroes: embraces and hugs and faces alive with delight at making our acquaintance. Every one of them had brought a gift, which he gave to the first student he came across. There was food, drink, juice, and cigarettes, even blankets. They all asked for news of their villages and friends. I was beside myself. I could have cuddled them all. But the governor's words rang in my ears. It wasn't beyond the bounds of possibility that one of them would trick me into letting my guard down and ravage me, so I huddled in a corner and resolved to have nothing to do with them.

Time for lockup came around, the doors were closed behind us, and we went to bed. In the morning we refused to eat breakfast. We only turned it down because we didn't like it and felt lazy but they thought it was a strike. The governor was deeply worried when he arrived but he quickly saw what was going on and ordered the food be improved. When lunch came we ate together then I crawled back to my blanket. A prisoner about fifty years old entered the cell carrying oranges in the lap of his gallabiya like a sack. He went around the students with his haul until he reached me. I declined the offer firmly and irritably and he pulled the hem of his robe over the oranges and beat a retreat.

The following day I awoke as soon as the doors were opened to hear a voice calling, "Anyone from the Fayoum in here?" I was about to reply, "Yes," but I swallowed it. He asked again and one of the students said, "Yes, we've got someone from the Fayoum," and pointed in my direction. Then came the inevitable, "You from the Fayoum?"

"No," I said.

"Yes you are. Where exactly?"

"From Itsa."

"Where in Itsa?"

"From al-Gharaq."

"Don't tell me you're from such and such a family?"

"I'm from such and such a family."

"Well, damn you, then. Why are you hunched up in the corner like that? We're neighbors! I'm from Minyat al-Hait, heard of it? I was locked up with some of your people in '83."

He listed the names of relatives of mine who were arrested during the course of a campaign against the al-Wahia tribe. "Come with me," he said, and I went. He took me to his cell, gave me a towel and some soap, and told me to take a shower, "and when you're done we'll have some breakfast." I washed and returned to the cell. He shared with four other men, all murderers, and their cell was neat and clean and equipped with all the amenities and luxuries you could wish for.

After that, I never left his side until the day I was released. We ate a delicious country breakfast: worm-cheese, mature white cheese, crispy bread, cucumber, tomato, and peppers. I started to relax and murmured my mother's favorite prayer: "May the hearts of the good salute you." I gave him the full account of my adventure from the arrest to sitting in front of him and he told me how he came to be imprisoned with my relatives. He had been unfairly treated, he said, but that was fate. The man with the oranges came in and said to me, "Scared of me, you idiot? Believe me, I'd fuck the blanket I sleep on if it started twitching, but you? Never." We all laughed and made up. He was a born comedian; he could get a laugh from a lump of stone. He worked as a burglar and spent his life either sitting in jail or breaking into apartments.

We would perform a little pantomime together that for some reason used to make me howl with laughter. Each time I met him I would say hello, and just as he was about to walk on I'd say, "Wait a moment, Amm Shehata," and carefully count my fingers, checking over and over again that they were all there. "Go ahead, Amm Shehata," I'd say, and we'd roar.

So: I never left his side—meaning, of course, my upstanding fellow countryman and his band of killers and pickpockets. Every morning, as soon as the doors were unlocked, he would bring me soap and a towel, present me with a box of Cleopatra Super cigarettes, and wait for me to join them over breakfast. I'd stay with him until lockup.

When they called my name for me to be released I was in his cell. I hugged him, and wept, and swore a terrible and binding oath that I would visit him constantly. I never did.

How Can I Call Out to You, Mother?

Until this point in my life I'd managed to hold myself together. Naturally, I'd been scared before—I'd almost died of fear—but I'd never gotten as far as blubbering and wailing. In the Beni Suef prison my self-control was even more unbreakable. The sheer length and gravity of my fellow prisoners' sentences, anywhere between life and a decade, made it easy for me to accept the idea of a year behind bars. I told myself I would use the time to retake my high school exams and improve my marks. Each morning I would bounce, bubbly and full of beans, over to the washroom (even humming on occasion), eat my breakfast, and spend the rest of the day swapping jokes with my neighbors. But when my mother came to visit I broke down. A deluge of all the feelings of indignity, humiliation, deprivation, and captivity that you could possibly imagine swept over me. Face-to-face meetings were forbidden. We were only permitted to look at our family members through the hatches in our cell doors. My mother was at the center of the crowd of visitors, but she couldn't see me. She was shading her eyes with her hands and moving from hatch to hatch. I couldn't think how to call her over, how to let her know that I was standing by the hatch of the third cell on floor three. Calling out to her over that distance was too embarrassing. Outside the cell, people swarmed like ants, while within I was surrounded by prisoners. What could I say? Mother? Mummy? It was mortifying. I thought of calling her by her name, but nothing came out. Why did I find it so hard to say? I almost choked trying. Finally, I asked a guy next to me to call out to her.

"See the woman with the black scarf over there? That one there. Call her over. Say, 'Over here! Your son's right here beside me.'"

We burst into tears.

Long, Smooth Fingers

I haven't been this agitated for a long time.

Why am I so confused and uncertain? Why do I waver between advance and retreat?

I'm all grown up.

I will die aged forty-five.

A madwoman with a nose ring and a tattoo on her face spat in my eye and said, "You'll die young. You won't live past forty-five." We were coming back from a match or a wedding, about ten of us, and the woman stopped us in the street. I don't know why I felt so proud. I looked at the other boys with the confidence of one who knows he has been somehow sanctified.

I was in junior high.

My first year of junior high.

I was nervous and bewildered and naïve.

I love. I yearn. I am tormented. In company I appear composed and competent: I do not love, I do not yearn, I am not tormented.

You could say that I was working against myself.

Against just what it was that I wanted.

And now,

As I write to you,

A call comes from home:

My cousin Walid . . . .

. . . wild, and on the verge of exploding into the receiver. "Hamdi!" he said, then, "Professor Hamdi . . ." and told me that our enemies (our tribe's enemies, that is) were about to achieve a sweeping victory. Our enemies are powerful, it's true, and intent on a scrap. Though short, our war with them has been packed with memorable incidents, memorable for them and for us. In the mountains we grind them into the dust. That's face to face on the field of battle, where the old laws still hold sway. They get us with the government, education, good jobs, and the law. My uncle beat up their leader, roped him to a palm tree, and dispensed the following poetic wisdom:

"When a dog grows fat, out come his incisors.

And he starts to savage friends and neighbors."

Their leader brought a court case against him, proved that he had sustained a grievous injury, and my uncle got three months. He milked it of course, moving through the villages with the swagger of a man who can get Bedouin sheikhs dragged off to jail. It was my uncle who made it all possible. We practically got down and kissed his feet, begging him to deny the charge, but he insisted that he had beaten him—precisely so he could boast that not only had he beaten him but he could do so again any time he chose.

Circumstances forced me into what I believe was our last confrontation with them. It was no longer possible to sustain these sorts of campaigns. Either they would have to submit to our numerical strength and history or we would have to accept their influence. I was impressed by their tenacious resolve to continue the fight, but the fact is they'd been strong from the beginning, holding powerful positions intimidating to a bunch of Bedouin who tend to steer clear of—indeed, actively fear—any form of interaction with the authorities.

It was the old story. We were an established Bedouin clan from the area (by area, I mean the narrow patch of land on which our squabble played out) and they were the only family to have arrived recently. Its founder used to tend sheep on my grandfather's land—not my great-grandfather, but the fifth in line, Grandfather Aula, my mother's father. This shepherd was a sharp, hard-working, serious-minded, and dedicated young man, perfect material for founding a family or a tribe. He knew full well that he was sowing seed in harsh and unforgiving soil, so he gave his boys (the intelligent ones, at least) the best education he could, while their contemporaries from our tribe could scarcely write. Furthermore, I don't share the rashness—or, shall we say, the courage—of my uncle, the one who bound his opponent to a palm tree, but I wish I did. It's so much more dignified than trying to prove that you are feared and respected in government circles.

Back to the matter in hand.

Our enemies, God protect us, were on the verge of victory . . . let them have it.

I was in love with my cousin.

Her name was Sahar.

I used to think it was Sahara and that the song "The Desert Comes to the Engineer" was written for us. She was the desert and I was the engineer. Still, I would try to show, and occasionally declare, that I was not in love with—indeed, didn't care about—my cousin. I was a member of that generous hearted company of men who believe that confessing love is a weakness and a humiliation. One can be loved, sure, but to love, to crawl around, to place oneself willingly on the scales like that, to be judged . . . ? No, a thousand times, no.

Do I still suffer from such beliefs?

Do I see in you another Sahar?

I was in junior high, and to my eyes love was nothing more than the challenge of confessing it. I needed Sahar to approach me, wink, and say the very things I would flinch from telling her.

Now I'm older. I've wept. I've said the words many times.

Do I lie? Of course I do.

The words "I love you" come easily when I don't mean them and they stick in my throat when I do.

And strange to say, the ones I've lied to have been attracted to me and have loved me far more than the poor wretches to whom honor forbade me from confessing my love.

One has more conviction, it seems, when unburdened by feelings, especially when they're real.

It's a dangerous road, plagued with doubt, confusion, worry, and fear.

These are our lives and we are free to do with them as we will.

Then we give it all up and wish we had not.

My cousin looked like the actress Raqia Ibrahim, especially her eyes. She was dynamic and dauntless and did what she wanted. Now she's a wife, a mother of seven, and if you saw her you'd call me a fool as others have done. But I like height, not imposing or looming or excessive, merely a higher height than is usual in a woman. (I'm very pleased with this "higher height" business: I had to think about it for a while.) Then there's slenderness. Slenderness, as the writers say, those bodies that invigorate rather than stimulate, that precipitate properties in a man of which he knew nothing. Every time I see you I groan; and not just every time I see you, but every time you come to mind, I try to recall your moans. Oh! How sweet they are, how magical, how desirable . . . .

It seems I am destined, victim of an inherent recklessness, to be swept away, to swap what is best for what is base, to sneer at the soul and sink into the flesh. The elevated and the honorable, all that circles in the firmaments of noble virtue I shall cast aside for what is low and lustful, for the historical sources of error and iniquity. I shall never be able to understand why man persecutes his physical form this way. I can't get to grips with it. I set out to convince you and here I am declaiming to mankind, but it's a fascinating subject. Look. Look around you. Why is everything forbidden to the body, while the soul stays free? You yourself, you leave your soul to frolic unchecked and chain your body, rein it in.

That's how we are. The lover who renders the body abstract, who numbs and paralyzes the flesh, we think superior to the lover who brings it to life. The former, we honor and respect. We admire him: we read his stories and memorize his verse. He was promised heavenly reward by the Prophet himself: "Whosoever loves and remains pure," he said, "shall enter Paradise." The latter is a criminal: accursed and foully slandered.

I, too, sent my soul to Sahar. I have no time for these figurative expressions but in deference to your theory of dispatching souls: I sent mine to Sahar. The difference is I wasn't playing around. If only I had been. I was joyful, I was depressed, I peered over the lip of madness, and all for things I later learned meant nothing to her. My soul, it seems, was lying to me, delivering false reports. I'd wander the whole village until at last I passed their house, just so no one could tell I had meant to; daily quests whose dogged determination astonishes me today. But the climax of my relationship with Sahar, the incident whose every detail is branded on my brain, took place elsewhere. We were at a wedding . . . . I clearly have a fondness for weddings: when I was boasting about my premonition of death I mentioned that we were returning from a wedding, and here I am meeting Sahar at a wedding. Did these weddings really take place, or has my inordinate penchant for the things caused me to picture it this way? You could consider it flattery or flirtation, or even an admission, that you, despite frustrations, have created something wonderful in my life. Even were we to part, to uncover, each one in turn, betrayal and start to war against each other, a sense of happiness, of joy, an ungovernable urge to laugh, will always remain.

Anyway: our village was awaiting one of its weddings. Weddings were our favored hunting ground: the whole village packed into a single place allowed for direct contact. I sat next to Sahar. She was sitting on a bench and I squeezed in beside her. I gave the matter some thought. An experienced friend had advised me to do as much.

"Don't waste your chance. At the wedding, sit next to her and stretch your hand out toward her hand without letting anyone see. Place your hand gently on her nearest finger. If she refuses—you know, pulls her hand away—then act like it was an accident. If she stays quiet . . . then congratulations, my friend."

I don't recall ever actually speaking to her, just wandering the village until I got the chance to spy on her house for a few seconds unobserved. Anyhow, I tried. She was wearing a dress, but I don't remember the color. I really made an effort but it wouldn't come. I'm in awe of those people who have a memory for color. I remember my cousin's dress, the length and the cut, and I remember that the hand on which my eye fell was framed in bangles, but not a single color.

Despite the lack of space her hand lay in the correct place. I watched and waited my chance. When it arrived I deposited my hand next to hers and let it creep slowly toward the ends of her fingers until it came to rest on top of them. I was ready for anything. If she pulled her hand away there was still plenty of time for me to pretend it was an accident, and if she didn't . . . then congratulations, my friend.

Umm Hassan

I am a graduate of the Umm Hassan College. That was its name. I got 50 percent in my high school exams and enrolled. It offered its alumni a rather bewildering educational qualification, better than mediocre and not quite good. Officially, the college fell within the purview of the Ministry of Higher Education. In reality—in terms of employment, marriage prospects, and social standing—their certificate carried the weight of a technical diploma. The students, esteemed colleagues one and all, were mostly poor and lazy. If we had been hardworking, or even mildly conscientious, we would have gotten into a public university. If we had been rich, or even moderately well-off, we would have gone to the private universities. It would be fair to say that Umm Hassan was attended exclusively by those completely lacking in enterprise and material support. The overwhelming majority were self-conscious about this and drew on their imaginations to better their situation. They would commonly refer to themselves as university students, or at least claim that they were "continuing their studies."

The diligent students among them may have been, but most had no idea what they were doing and simply drifted along aimlessly. I worked in Shubra for a while, then for Mi'allim Matar, and waited. The college was notorious in northern Upper Egypt—throughout the entire region for all I know—for its indecency, or, shall we say, its moral laxity. It was named after a woman from Beni Suef who ran a bordello nearby (or, it was alleged, inside the college).

Courses there lasted two years. The first few months of the first year were a nightmare. I would have wild visions in my sleep and piss myself. Come the middle of the night I would be falling off mountains and buildings, toppling from the backs of titanic beasts. Awake, I would make excuses. I'd tell people, my family in particular, that I was retaking my high school exams. To this day, I try and avoid talking about my academic qualifications. Whenever a friend starts reminiscing about his student years I become depressed, depressed and embarrassed, and I use all my powers of misdirection and eloquence to change the subject. For all that it was notoriously ignorant, our village regarded Umm Hassan as a mark of failure. To go to secondary school and get everybody used to treating you as a bright young boy, only to end up at Umm Hassan: this meant you had let the village down. A tough old aunt of mine still criticizes me in front of my mother. Ill-starred and illiterate she may be, but it doesn't stop her leaning back and declaring, "It's a college for donkeys."

Umm Hassan is located in Beni Suef, a region it closely resembles in that it's the focus of slur and slander throughout Upper Egypt. Everything in Beni Suef is back to front: the men sleep at home and the women go out to work. They roll up their sleeves and set to in the fields or walk the streets. It's an ambivalent place, too. It is not well known for anything, like the other governorates are. Geographically and administratively it belongs to northern Upper Egypt and lies about 150 kilometers south of Cairo. With respect to behavior and customs and way of life in general, however, it has nothing to do with Upper Egypt or Cairo. The dialect itself is an elastic, formless hybrid of Cairene and Bedouin. When a Cairene wants to ask where something is, he says "fein," and the Bedouin, "wein." The inhabitants of Beni Suef (and the Fayoum, as well) say "faaa." The Cairene says "da" for "that" and the Bedouin says "hadda," but the Beni Suefi says "deeda."

Save those on whom God has taken pity, all its inhabitants (not just the men) are miserable wretches of legendary gauntness and helplessness. They remind you of those unfortunates mentioned by the Most High, the ones over whom ignominy and destitution were set and who drew upon themselves the terrible wrath of God. They swamp the day labor market in Cairo and flagrantly undercut the other workers. It's the classic story. The customer or the contractor goes to the market—the bridge or the public square where the laborers wait for work—and starts negotiating with an Upper Egyptian. The Upper Egyptian tells him a day's work is twenty pounds and refuses to budge. His fellow worker from Beni Suef or the Fayoum suddenly pokes his head forward, servile and groveling, and proclaims, "I'll do it for five, your worship."

Beni Suef is the only governorate in Egypt where women exercise near absolute authority, an authority lacking only official representation such as high-ranking public positions. Women deserve to run the place. In fact it's about the only province where people wouldn't be surprised to find a woman in charge. Women are everything there. They hold executive power and it's their counsel that prevails. I myself have lived in seven houses owned, managed, and terrorized by women.

Beni Suef, capital of Beni Suef governorate, is a small town. Umm Hassan is one of its most famous educational establishments and most attractive to non-local students. Though some departments of Cairo University had branches in town the Umm Hassan building was always the most crowded. It resembled an ancient but unassuming palace, three floors high and surrounded by iron railings. Its builder—clearly no expert when it came to palaces—had given it a huge number of rooms at the expense of any grand halls and chambers. The ancient fabric of the building was cracked and rusted throughout. It would have been a profitable renovation job for Matar. I would sometimes think it out for him. No more than two hundred meters square: ten men maximum. Dig out and reinforce the foundations then pour and erect the load-bearing columns. Two months in all, sixty days, maybe less, and these three floors you're looking at would be five. Seven, even.

They say it was nationalized in the 1960s and that it became a high school before it was turned into Umm Hassan. After passing through the iron gateway the first sight to greet you is a broad marble staircase leading directly to the second floor, a staircase associated with what I regard as an important day both in my life and the history of Beni Suef as a whole. The Brothers and I were descending the staircase in a panic, having expressed our views on the President, the government, Israel, and the world in general ("Coward! Agent of the Americans!") . . . .

So: the old palace first, then the historic staircase sweeping upward immediately beyond the gate. In view of the increasing numbers of entrants a second building was hastily erected, and between the two buildings stretched a narrow yard where I, during my months of self-imposed isolation (I almost wrote preparation), paced out yards and yards each day. It was like a catwalk: girls of every stamp and hue, the veiled and the shameless. I was experiencing difficulties with my appearance. My face in particular was a problem. I felt, and still do, that it was an old face, and one that excited hostile responses in onlookers. Severe, watchful, and menacing, it failed to convey the true nature of my feelings. The moment I turned my attention to a girl she would get up in alarm and sometimes walk away. Perhaps, I thought, things might improve if I made certain adjustments to its features. For a while I followed the example of soccer players in the 1970s (naturally, I am not referring to the shorts and afros but that air of dissipated cool that made the face look both distracted and condescending). To this end I would scrub my teeth with sand, curl my lip with an insolence befitting their brilliance, and stroll among the girls at the college in the hope that one of them would be taken by the sight.

The female students from the towns were neat, elegant, and liberated and I quickly saw that they were the exclusive property of their urban comrades. The country girls were boulders of inanimate rock. You had to physically assault them before they'd notice you. In such circumstances my wanderings proved fruitless. I tried with everyone. I scraped my teeth and purchased vast quantities of hair oil. I had a go at every single one of the campus beauties, without exception. I observed them for days, gazing in admiration, smiling and winking, and when they finally lost patience, I switched my attentions to a girl from back home. She was from the Fayoum and she was tough. Tall and broad, the epitome of serious mindedness, she diligently attended all her lectures and classes, though this had little impact on her understanding or marks. She first attracted my attention by stopping in front of another student in the cafeteria, yawning hugely, then slapping him sharply across the back of the neck.

He was one of those students who came to college just to chase the girls, and furthermore he was a hippie. I disliked him intensely and I respected her. I felt that we could easily get together. Conditions were favorable. Normally, I don't have much time for conditions and compromise and the misshapen types it brings with it. Only the prettiest girls catch my eye, which has naturally brought me my fair share of disappointments, though there's no need to go into them here. She'll be an experiment, I said, a bit of training on my level. She might improve my standing among the other girls in the college, though I'm not sure why I expected a man would become more attractive merely by having a girlfriend, especially one like her. We would exchange looks all day. If one of us caught the other at it they would turn their face away and do their best to appear disgusted and scornful. We almost sneered. I was unable to forget that I was the only student who had made a pass at her and she was likewise unable to forget that she was the only female student who had responded to my advances.

It was during my pursuit of this and other girls that the prospect of repeating my high school exams began to seem ever more unappealing. Another year to be frittered away pointlessly. I came across others like me, frustrated by college and life. We formed a gang. Naji and Najih were Bedouin from Minya, Abd al-Wanis and myself Bedouin from the Fayoum.

Beni Suef was the first town I lived in on a permanent basis. I went to primary school in our village, junior high and high school in a neighboring village, and my trips up to Cairo were fleeting, a week or two at most before rushing back to mummy. Before I met them I was ashamed of myself. My accent was a particularly heavy burden. I would try to give the impression that I was a city boy, bending my tongue and flexing my lips, but it was no use. The moment I uttered a word everybody became fully aware that I was a Bedouin from the Fayoum countryside. Times had changed, I was forced to explain. Camels, tents, and burkas were a thing of the past. The Bedouin were civilized. They occupied important positions in the police and the army and the judiciary. I would usually invoke the name of my relative, Dr. Abu Bakr Yusif, translator of Chekhov and editor of the works of Dostoevsky. "He's one of us," I'd say, "You know: my uncle."

Having met them, I grew bolder. I began openly harassing the students of Beni Suef. I realized that I possessed qualities to be proud of. My accent, for instance: its very obscurity was an advantage. More often than not people will respect you, and might even fear you, if you speak a language they can't understand. As time passed I began to assert my identity shamelessly. Sometimes I would come to college wearing the shanna, the Bedouin headdress of the Western deserts from Egypt to Morocco, and a woolen cloak. I'd swell with pride when we held a conversation in the Bedouin dialect within hearing of our fellow students. My strategy for dealing with girls changed. In place of the furtive shiftiness I found so enervating I allowed my face to reassume its natural shape. With the intention of molesting them, of course, I would barrel right into them, occasionally abusing them in Bedouin dialect. All the students, even the rural ones, wolf-whistled and hissed at girls, but it was all "What an angel," and "Hey darling." I would actually abuse them. It's an old habit of mine, and I've since come across precedents for this practice in Libya and the Gulf where we have our roots. When a man over there sees an attractive woman on the street and is tempted to flirt with her he will let loose a stream of invectives ("Move it, whore!"). I was at the same primary school as a female relative of mine. I was head over heels in love with her. Every day I would scribble messages to her on lampposts and walls. Not messages, really, more a mind-numbing artillery bombardment of abuse. I'm too embarrassed to write them here. Sometimes, though, I'd get myself in trouble. Once I told a girl, "You look like a duck coming back from market." It was all the rage at the time. But she replied, with a disdain I'm all too familiar with, "And you're a dog with no tail."

Our gang was together constantly, at college and at home. I gave up on the idea of retaking my high school exams and my fear of wasting another year and I began to live. That's what I was doing when the demonstration took place. I entered a short story competition open to all the technical colleges and won twenty pounds. I can't remember if it was a consolation prize or recognition for coming in the top three, but it came at the right time. We had lunch together, bought four packs of Cleopatra cigarettes, and calculated how much I'd make if I sold all my stories. Of them all, I was closest to Naji. We entered the Beni Suef General Prison together. I visited him in Minya and he came to see me in the Fayoum. At college we moved as a unit. Hostility, even proximity, to one of us meant an attack on us all. We spent the whole time sniffing after the girls—in the cafeteria, by the classroom doors—trying to get their attention by shouting: shrieks, laughs, and high-fives on the flimsiest of pretexts. And never a single glance.

We would meet up, make a round of the college, get a cup of tea in the cafeteria, and then head back to our residences. We would give the Brothers a wide berth. If they asked us to pray we would pray, and we experienced a sense of shared satisfaction when they beat up one or other of the security guards. They were exceptionally active. About twenty students embarked on a campaign to purge the college. They held prayer sessions, encouraged the wearing of the veil, and prevented male students standing with the girls. Now and again they succeeded in getting groups of students to march around chanting, "Our college is a college of heroes, we won't take being treated like zeroes." They would have run-ins with the dean, or the "font of all corruption" to use their phrase, confronting him during lectures and accusing him of working for the security services. The security services would duly intervene and a Brother would suddenly disappear for a week or two only to return and strut around the campus a hero. Which is what I thought of them: heroes. Anyone who could enter the Beni Suef State Security Directorate and emerge in one piece was a hero by any standard. One Thursday, January 5 1987, one of the Brothers came up to me and said, "We're having a demonstration today. Some Brothers have been arrested by state security. You ready?"

We were quite well-known. The way we looked, the clothes we wore, and our Bedouin dialect had won us some small notoriety, but on the whole we kept to ourselves. We didn't join any societies or groups and we ignored the student union. We did follow events, though, such as the battles between the two main student groups: on one side the union of students comprised of the Lotus, Horus, and Mosaic fraternities and the like, and on the other, the Brothers. These clashes usually took place during the season of field trips and organized excursions. The fraternities would demand juicy outings with girls and boys together, while the Brothers preferred their excursions dry, and out would come the knives and bike chains. The fraternities were the establishment, supported by the dean, and the Brothers were the opposition, but they were the most powerful opposition I've ever seen in my life. They practically ran the college. When the debate over the excursions reached boiling point they kicked the dean's door off its hinges and he almost died of fright. The excursions were organized in accordance with Islamic law: one trip for the Brothers, another for the Sisters.

Extremely Tall

Abu Antar, the owner of my building in Ain Shams was originally from Upper Egypt, from Qena, I think. He traveled to Saudi Arabia and lived like a monk for ten years until he had saved enough to buy a house. He was extremely tall. You don't see many that tall in a lifetime. He usually wore a gallabiya on bare skin and wrapped his head in a turban that was sometimes gleaming white and sometimes filthy. He suffered from a speech impediment and hated talking. When he spoke it was like he was swallowing or vomiting. His Adam's apple would get into difficulties, rising and falling with astonishing speed, and he would fall back on gesticulation. When he growled, threw up his hands, and shook them, we would know that he was angry. He was always angry. Our loitering by the window, our many visitors, our incessant laughter: all were met by his flapping hands. We would see him on the stairs in a state of never-ending labor, carrying things upstairs and down. He would swing sacks and planks and, sometimes, live animals onto his shoulder and climb, his face to the floor and his gallabiya sweeping the stairs. At first we would greet him. "Good morning," we'd say, or, "Keep going," but experience taught us to rely on his language. We growled, he growled, and each went his separate way.

He compensated for his lack of speech by eavesdropping on his tenants, and on us in particular. He wasn't eavesdropping exactly. That implies you are pretending to ignore people while listening to what they are saying, and he never ignored anybody. He merely had an excessively broad interpretation of a landlord's proper rights and powers. It was his right to know what was going on; besides which, we were strangers and unmarried and God alone knew what we were getting up to in his house.

During his trips up and down the stairs he would select a door, lean his entire body against it, and slowly lower his ear until it covered the keyhole. Sometimes he'd be bent beneath the weight of some heavy load, and if a tenant happened to open their door he would fix him with a look of intense disapproval and innocently continue on his way. He fell into our room numerous times. We would open the door to find him hunched over the keyhole. On one occasion he was carrying a sack. He growled, we growled, and he turned around to continue his climb. The Doctor was with me and the sack was clearly very heavy, a hundred kilos or so. We saw how hard it was for him to stand up but he didn't ask for any help. His gallabiya was hoisted up over his shoulders to protect the back of his neck. He shook slightly, feeling for the nearest step with his right foot, then his left. Carefully, he began to climb.

At that time we were more or less enemies. We would growl fiercely and he would respond with a growl twice as fierce. He was waiting for a chance to kick us out, or so we understood from his tone. We needed to make a peace offering. At the end of the day it was his house and he could invade our room at any time. The Doctor and I exchanged a look that said we must seize the opportunity. His hands were clamped on the edges of the sack and some feeling of irritation or embarrassment seemed to be confusing his steps. I grabbed the Doctor and we caught up with him. Together we lifted the sack off his backside. He neither objected nor consented, but continued upward as if nothing had happened. Suddenly, his trousers fell down. They were white and baggy and from Saudi Arabia where he'd bought them back in the days of scrimp and save. One of us must have trodden on them, or maybe the elastic gave way. One moment they were round his buttocks and the next they were trailing between his feet. His bottom, perhaps from shame, was tightly clenched and looked like a mouth that had lost its teeth. I would never have guessed he had such a delightful bottom. Not skin on bone, but skin stretched across two hard muscles.

The Doctor tried to cover him up. He growled a warning to the old man and tried repeatedly to lift the trousers, but Abu Antar climbed grimly on until we reached the roof. His wife was up there. It was the first time we had seen her. She looked as though she had come straight from an Upper Egyptian funeral: black headdress, black gallabiya, and a worked nose-ring of gold or perhaps brass—I couldn't tell. The rooftop was littered with pieces of wood and metal and a large number of objects, some disintegrating, some intact, and sorted according to type. He led us, or rather dragged us, to the corner where the sacks were stacked; he a powerful truck, we the trailer. Half the sack rested on his neck and the other half lay in our hands. Suddenly, without so much as a growl, he abdicated his half of the sack, causing us to almost fall over. Stumbling, we came to rest against a wall and waited for him to go off and cover himself up, but he just stood there naked, his penis a monkey crouched in a jungle. Before we could put the sack down he growled and muttered to himself.

"We're filthy," said his wife.

Abu Tahoun

Our village is always on my mind. From my very first day in Shubra I thought of it as my true home, the only place where I move free from fear, a citizen with rights and obligations. I place it before me and leaf through its memories, those histories of a wounded homeland. Why I always associate homelands with injury I could not say. They seem somehow more impressive, more authentic, when debilitated by wounds. And our village is wounded: poor and tiny, set far from the highway and the market and fresh water, and surrounded on every side by the desert. There's an old legend about the place that its neighbors like to tell, which goes something like this.

Moses asked his Lord, "Lord, is there anywhere poorer than al-Abaaj?"

"Come now, Moses," replied the Lord in a mournful yet heavenly timbre, "Abu Tahoun is poorer still . . . ."

Al-Abaaj is a hamlet affiliated to us both tribally and administratively, and Abu Tahoun (official name, Daniel, after the Prophet Daniel) is our village. The words of the poet—"Ours is a fearful and unforgiving land"—were written for Abu Tahoun. Its inhabitants are Bedouin tribesmen and peasants, its produce the crops and animals we tend. It has scant agricultural land: strips of green stretching serpent-like into the wastes. It was granted to our grandparents by Mohamed Ali Pasha in the days of forced settlement. Early on, the Pasha realized that there was no chance of founding a modern state with the Mamluks and Bedouin around. The Mamluks he slaughtered. The Bedouin he settled . . . and slaughtered. Let's just say he settled the Bedouin who were willing to be settled and slaughtered those willing to be slaughtered. But all that takes time to explain; let's stay with Abu Tahoun.

The Bedouin own the land and the peasants work it. There may not be much of it, but Bedouin don't farm. There is only one power in the village: the Bedouin are the rulers and the peasants are the ruled and things are stable. Small and poor though our village is and far from locations of strategic importance it may be, but its headman exercises control over nine villages, the smallest of which—in terms of geographical size, population, and income—dwarfs our own. Abu Tahoun's inhabitants, Bedouin and peasants alike, move among their neighbors as if each and every one were a headman, lords and masters of all they survey. Of course, as is the fate of rulers everywhere, we are exposed to ridicule. The inhabitants of the villages—the homelands—that surround us have countless contemporary stories to add to the tale of Moses and his Lord. They say we are cold, that we speak slowly, that we have no fire in our bellies. They say we're greedy and idle, that we're full of empty words—that our very lives are nothing more than empty words.

For the most part, the inhabitants of our village, Bedouin and peasant alike, never rush to the defense of their home. They are content to soak up their neighbors' slanders in silence, a silence that amounts to encouragement. True, one of us occasionally might get angry and make something of it, but most seem perfectly content. Personally, I see nothing worth defending. The name alone is suspect: a miserable tomb, a ruined stone sentinel ringed by a dilapidated wall. It's not even clear whether its occupant, "Saint Daniel," was Christian or Muslim. Having thought about it, I figure it's a place you flee from, or at best a stopover, a staging post for passing travelers. I'm pretty sure that when my forebears dismounted here they were intending to stretch their legs, not stay forever.

I have been fervent in my time, been gripped by feelings of local pride, led rallies and rumbles whenever our village team played our neighbors. I have earnestly prayed to God that we might beat them and swelled with the purest feelings of pride when we defeated them in their own back yard. I have been first to join the militias when our village came under attack from outsiders. I've spent long nights readying ambushes and bandages and waiting for the chance to destroy the foe. There were about ten of us, young men eager and ready to die (if it came to it) for the sake of ideas like glory, honor, and the blood of the tribe. Nothing frustrated us, nor tested our resolve more, than young men intent on stealing our women. The law of our village states that peasants may not marry Bedouin girls and we were zealous champions of this law. So we'd bide our time and lay traps, but the enemy (and this type in particular) would never engage us face to face. They'd slip our snares and ambushes and come morning we'd hear the news: so-and-so has given his daughter away to a peasant.

It seems that I have lost my way again. I should be talking about my homeland. Now Abu Tahoun is small, and perhaps insignificant compared to a proper homeland, but it's the only place where I move free from fear, a citizen with rights and obligations. Whenever I visit, even now, I try to make them understand how successful I've been, to make it crystal clear that I have achieved a degree of leverage in the city, in the enemy's back yard. I have no need of leverage when I live in their midst, but I've never found a better place to help me understand the true extent of my powers. I welcome them into a living room carpeted with newspapers and magazines and move the conversation toward politics, the better to introduce the topic of my successes: the writing and the publishing; the dream I'm living in Cairo. I once told one of them I was an "author." We'd been smoking and I felt I could trust him. "By the way," I said, "I've got four books out: two lots of short stories, a novel, and a collection of odds and ends."

Both I and they are in constant need of protection, not from enemies immediately at hand, but from more distant foes: the police and the government. I'm currently trying to make them understand that my Cairene exile has not been time wasted, that an "author" is no mean protection. He is a man capable of reprimanding, even of abusing, police officers and can push open, and on occasion kick down, the doors of government officials.

I came to Cairo at the beginning of the seventies and stayed until midway through the decade. I worked for a while as a laborer, and my fellow villagers and I would keep to ourselves. We would walk the streets of Cairo but as sons of another, distant country, to which we awaited the chance to return. And now, when I make the journey to the village, I say, "I'm going home": returning to my homeland.

Bakr

Mi'allim Bakr was from back home. His full name: Bakr Qarani Bayoumi. He came to Cairo earlier than most. He was short, solid, and always elegantly attired in an Alexandrian gallabiya and glowing white turban; in winter he added a cashmere shawl and woolen robe. Whatever the weather he was never without a pressed white skullcap. A font of stories, of boasts unending, and epic tales of his exploits and the heroics of others, he came to the city as a simple workman in the sixties. But he strived and struggled and learned how to be a plasterer. He founded a famous crew, twenty plasterer-skimmers, which only worked in the classiest neighborhoods. He worked as a subcontractor for an engineering firm in Mohandiseen and did very well out of it. The firm offered him opportunities that would have made anyone else but Bakr a rich man. He still sighs over the land that was offered to him for pennies and now changes hands for millions. Although his work was in Cairo, he never settled there. He'd spend a week or two in the buildings where he had jobs then return to his children in the village. When he needed a place to stay he'd take a two-room bachelor apartment anywhere he could find it. He would try not to employ workers from the village. The most irritating thing about them was their habit of treating him as though they were back in the village. They failed to give him the respect due to a contractor, crew boss, and provider of gainful employment. I was the only one who worked with him regularly and we had something like a father-son relationship. Each week we would travel to the village and return together. I stayed with him in a two-bedroom place in Kafr al-Jabal the time he was working on the Maryoutiya project: ten buildings overlooking Faisal Street where we'd work all day and sleep at night. If we were working two week-long shifts in a row he'd buy a kilo of meat from a famous butcher in Doqqi, I'd cook it with rice or pasta, and we'd spend our Thursday and Friday listening to the Sira Hilaliya, the epic of the Hilal tribe. He lived for the Sira, and through the long night he would vie with the tape recorder for the honor of narrating it to me.

For a while I supervised twenty plasterers for Bakr and I became friends with some of them, none more so than the senior skimmer—their "commander"—Khalaf. He was tall and thin and in poor health but he was an artist, specializing in ornamental decorations and designs. We were more than friends; we ran the crew together, overseeing the plasterers and handing them their wages when Bakr wasn't around. Now and then he'd take me with him on outside repair jobs, to palaces and villas where his creativity could find true expression. It was while we were working together that he was laid low by a mysterious back problem something in his spine. I found this intensely upsetting. I wrote a melancholy short story about him entitled *Qitharatu Khalafi-l-bannaa'i*, or "The Guitar of Khalaf the Builder," but due to my ignorance of proper voweling it was published as *Qitharatun khalfa-l-binaa'i*, "A Guitar Behind the Building." Khalaf himself understood it as a formal complaint on his behalf, an eloquent plea directed at senior officials to get the state to pay for his treatment. Almost daily he would ask me, "So, they haven't replied? No one got back to you?"

I wrote a story about Bakr as well, but befitting his elevated status it was slightly more philosophical in approach. I tried to turn him into my father, something I have no experience of myself. I still don't know the correct tone, the appropriate sonic formulation, for the phrase "my father." I'm always experimenting on my own—Pa, Pops, Daddy—yet nothing seems to work. For a while there I made an effort to find myself a real father, a dad I could be ashamed of, that I could fear, a man for whom I'd move heaven and earth. I've tried it with all the great men I've known, or shall we say, the men who have given me protection and love, of whom Bakr, of course, was one. At work, at home, even back in the village, I would treat him as if he were my father. For his part, unfortunately, he could never quite take me seriously. I couldn't take myself seriously. I felt like a fake, a liar, a hypocrite. The plasterers viewed the whole affair with considerable mistrust, as it confirmed their suspicions that I might be the "boss's bitch," his extra pair of eyes in their midst.

I was nineteen and studying at the college. My task was to prepare the plaster and water for twenty plasterer-skimmers scattered around a ten-story building. I'd wake at five and by the time the plasterers arrived at eight I would've prepared a bowl of plaster for each team of four and put a barrel of water on each floor. The work was regular and guaranteed. Mi'allim Bakr's crew was professionally run, with a head and feet, not like the mess in Shubra. You worked a full week and got your pay on Thursday. I would hand the wages to the craftsmen and laborers: a workman during the week and an accountant on Thursdays. Every now and then, every fortnight or so, I'd take a nice little sum back to the village. I'd rub oil and white spirit into my neck and hands to wipe away the last traces of plaster and cement, put on a clean, pressed gallabiya, and spend the holiday at home posing as a man of importance, playing the village intellectual to a tee. Rising late, towel slung over my shoulder I would make my way down to the canal bank, toothbrush and toothpaste held aloft, then sit all day on the bench leafing through books and reading not a word.

The drawback of working for Bakr's crew was that it was real work, day and night. You'd work in the buildings during the day and, at night, sleep there with your co-workers on collapsing beds made out of off-cuts and cement sacks. I came to resent it even more when the only time I actually did go out I was arrested. I was wearing a gallabiya and my beard had grown out and I was sitting with a colleague at a café at the end of Faisal Street. A police officer pulled up in his van and pulled us into the Haram police station for questioning, along with a sizeable number of people from the café and the street outside. The experience was considerably more difficult and frightening for me because it was only a few months since I'd been imprisoned for demonstrating. I was terrified that they'd find out and then I'd be in for it. The cells were packed and when we came in, one of the prisoners—clearly their leader—said, "Hold it, you two. Empty your pockets."

"We don't have anything," I told him firmly. "We work as laborers."

This was a serendipitous choice of words. "Sit down," he said, "Get on the floor." I stayed quiet, cleared myself some space, squirmed around until I could support my head with my arm, and finally slept. I awoke to interrogation. I heard the screams and sobs of everyone who had gone in before me and was petrified. I pictured punches and kicks, slaps, and fingers up my ass: the standard set of horrors. I prayed to God with all my heart.

"O Most Wise of Rulers," I said to Him, "just save me today then do with the remainder of my life what you will."

I recited all the prayers and charms that protect a man from evil and harm. And I was heard. I passed before an officer without him noticing me at all. *We have covered them so that they do not see.* I went out into the street and left Bakr's crew that very day. I took off. I hated its stifling atmosphere. Shubra is better by far; Shubra is life. There we work with people, in the midst of stable, happy families. Shubra is work and play.

Fayoum

I got to know the town of Fayoum quite late. I'm originally from the governorate of the Fayoum, from Abu Tahoun, which lies about forty kilometers to the south of town. Of course, I'd go there to catch buses to Cairo and elsewhere. In junior high and high school I would visit in order to eat felafel sandwiches in Katkout restaurant on al-Mohamediya Street, koshari in Sukkar on Mustafa Pasha Street, and to go to the cinema—in winter, Fayoum cinema next to the old Palace of Culture, and in summer the Abd al-Hamid cinema by Bahr Yusif. They were the only two cinemas in Fayoum, and if you ever get a chance to see them and the two restaurants I mentioned you'll have a fair idea of our circumstances at the time. Katkout was down a very narrow alley, about half a meter wide and four meters in length. It closed down years ago and has been replaced by a shoe shop, but it served the most delicious sandwiches I've eaten in my life. Sukkar is still there. A visit to Sukkar was, in itself, reason enough to boast to your friends and neighbors, though I can't recall what it was we found so attractive about the place. It was cramped, dirty, and stifling and resembled nothing more than a train terminal for flies. Incidentally, the flies of Fayoum are legendary for their courage, their persistence, their belligerence, and their size. The Abd al-Hamid cinema was covered in netting and was closed down after it subsided onto the audience, many of whom were badly hurt and had to be taken to the hospital. The two cinemas were popular destinations for the youth of Abu Tahoun and neighboring villages. I have a cousin who watched *Take Care of Zouzou* starring Soad Hosni twice a day for a whole fortnight at the Abd al-Hamid cinema and was among those injured when it collapsed.

Yet Fayoum was no more than a glorified station. It either set us on the great highways leading north, or carried us back to the villages in the south. We left and returned in groups, in gaggles, students and itinerant workers, boarding at the train station in Hamad Pasha Square. To our ears the squealing of the train's wheels conveyed a message clear as day. As the train left the station for distant lands it said, "Cheese and worms, cheese and worms . . ." and as it returned, "Cake and sugar, cake and sugar . . . ."

On my first visit to Fayoum I was in primary school. In those days (the 1970s to the early 1980s) the remains of the city of Shedet, ancient capital of the Fayoum, could still be seen around the region of Kiman Faris, a place of marshes, papyrus, halfa grass, and reeds, where statues and obelisks lay abandoned in the mire. As the years went by it vanished beneath the Kiman Faris apartment blocks.

I went with my mother. Confronted by my persistent pleas, backed up by many hot tears and angry stamping of feet, she took me with her to al-Miarrash Street, a covered marketplace specializing in textiles and cheap shoes. It's still going today, the main street giving off into narrow alleys crowded with furniture workshops. Most, if not all, of the furniture currently found in the homes of Fayoum's villages comes from here. Sadly, I remember nothing of the visit save the spitting incident. Walking along near al-Miarrash Street it entered my head to look up and examine the buildings around me. At the same moment it occurred to a local resident to spit downward. A cannonball of phlegm fell right into my eye: hot, sticky, and larger than any I had ever spat or seen myself.

For my next visit I was still in primary school and we were buying my eldest sister's trousseau. Prancing gleefully behind my mother I was assaulted by a local boy of about my age who plunged a pin into my back and vanished. I screamed at the top of my voice and my mother nearly had a heart attack. She thought I'd been bitten by a snake.

My mother associates Fayoum with snakebites. She first went there in the fifties with my father. At that time the town consisted of some markets, a public hospital, two or three palaces, and a number of government offices and residential buildings by Bahr Yusuf (which has since been filled in). Only the poor neighborhoods were busy, places like Sheikh Hassan and Sheikha Shifa, where the majority of the houses were built from mud brick. My mother and father were newlyweds and had yet to hear of electricity. They went to the hospital. Electricity reached the Fayoum in 1926, and it took a full fifty years more to reach our villages. The doctor was taking his time and my mother, irritated, yawned and stretched, a little too far as it turned out. Unfurling her arms to their fullest extent her hand brushed an exposed wire in a nearby socket. She screamed at the top of her voice, "Abu Hamid! A snake!"

"Where? Where is it?" gasped my father, and she pointed toward the socket. "In that rock," she said and gave the violent shudder of the authentic snakebite victim. Abu Hamid vengefully raised his staff and would have set about pulverizing the snake's lair had not a passing citizen explained to him that it was in fact electricity and not a snake. My mother saw her first television on the same trip and conveyed news of these two miracles back to the village. She told our goggle-eyed neighbors about the electric demon that stings like a snake and the black box full of tiny people who accost you and speak to you.

Years afterward my father went back to Fayoum to work as a guard and took my mother with him. They lived in a room near the covered market. At that point I hadn't even been thought of and the relationship between the town's residents and the Bedouin who lived all around them was still somewhat tense. The Fayoumis regarded the Bedouin as a bunch of thuggish bandits, while the Bedouin thought of them as peasants that no purebred Bedouin would consider talking to, let alone marrying. Until the 1940s, the Bedouin made their living from robbery and theft, plundering the towns and villages of the Fayoum with dependable regularity. They only participated in the revolution of 1919 and risked imprisonment to revenge themselves on behalf of their cousin, Hamad Pasha al-Basil, and continue their pillaging and looting along acceptable (i.e., revolutionary) principles after the government had successfully neutralized them by subjecting them to two successive slaughters in the villages of the Itsa municipality in the southern Fayoum.

Incidentally, the 1919 revolution in the Fayoum was nothing like its counterpart in Cairo. Naguib Mahfouz and the directors that brought his famous trilogy to the silver screen depict modern young men in suits and ties marching through the streets of Cairo brandishing the crescent and the cross and chanting, "We die, we die, and Egypt lives!" The British were happy to oblige them by way of bullets fired from the balconies of the Qasr al-Nil barracks. There was no chanting in the Fayoum, merely a mild hubbub and the nonstop looting of railway lines and government offices and the severing of telephone cables. They attacked police stations and carried off everything inside. Despite the large number imprisoned or slain by the English the revolutionary courts did not subsequently treat them as revolutionaries or resistance fighters who had sacrificed their lives for the nation but as a mob of petty crooks and bandits. But that's another story . . . .

To resume: our relationship with Fayoum's inhabitants remained tense until the 1970s or eighties (maybe it still is) and violent confrontations were common. Suffice to say, the educated and civilized town-dwellers grew tired of fighting with a bunch of oafs from the wilderness whose only obvious talent was wielding clubs and guns. Impoverished Bedouin had been descending on Fayoum since the early forties in search of employment, the work the town's cultured denizens declined, such as manual labor, laying sewage pipes and electricity cables, and guarding agencies and institutions both public and private.

My father worked as a security guard at a private school in the center of town. Due to his ignorance of the habits and customs of Fayoum he went to live in the house of a woman who earned her living from prostitution. Egypt abolished officially sanctioned prostitution in the 1940s, but in Fayoum it remained alive and well up until the sixties. My father could have held his peace and taken my mother to live in another neighborhood, but he chose instead to run back to the village and return accompanied by a band of men bristling with guns and fighting staffs. They destroyed the house, turned it upside down. He was arrested, held for a few days in the cells of the Fayoum police station, and when he was released took a new home on Mustafa Pasha Street in downtown Fayoum.

One morning, performing his appointed duties outside the school, he came face to face with the singer Sabah, the most famous person he had ever seen in his life. She was in town to open a festival of song at the Auberge in celebration of Fayoum's national holiday. Pulling up next to him in her vast automobile she asked him where to find the Auberge and he gestured indifferently in the right direction. Sabah was clearly taken with his appearance, awestruck by this living dinosaur with his shanna and Bedouin dialect. Either that, or his feigned indifference to her presence irritated her. Anyway, she disembarked from the vehicle, politely greeted him, and said, "I'm Sabah. Don't you know who I am?" hoping that he would show some sign of animation. When he remained motionless she offered to let him ride with her to the Auberge and take whatever he wanted in return. She would put a word in with the mayor to transfer him to a better job. He declined with maximal disdain and from that day forward was celebrated in Abu Tahoun and the surrounding villages as the man who turned down Sabah when she offered herself to him.

My relationship with Fayoum deepened in the eighties. For a while I lived in a friend's apartment in a run-down residential block in the neighborhood of Quhafa, home to Fayoum's middle classes. There was an art school in the neighborhood where I would congregate with other young men to ogle the girls. I joined the Literary Club in the Old Cultural Palace: two apartments in a slowly crumbling building. I heard the tales—or rather, the divine miracles—of Sheikh Omar Abd al-Rahman, who used to preach at the mosque under the noses of State Security agents and then walk the streets surrounded by a throng of supporters. State Security was unable to arrest him due to the press of people and the multitude of blind doubles dressed like the Sheikh. Each time they thought they'd finally arrested the sightless sage and each time their victim would tell them he was a look-alike and that the sly old fox had fled to Asyut or Minya or some other place.

I got invited into the homes of the local inhabitants. Whether they had been born there or arrived later in life they were for the most part impoverished and downtrodden. The historian Othman al-Nablusi, author of *Fayoum and Its Countryside*, hit the nail on the head when he described them as layabouts "who do not move unless pushed and possess no nobility, virtue, dignity, bravery, or merit."

The Room in Ain Shams

The room—the room in Ain Shams—was on the third floor. All on its own and free from the tyranny of the other apartments, the last step on the staircase meant you had arrived, that you were now standing before my books, the gas stove, and the blankets Daniel had bought for us. Truth be told, he had bought them for himself. His room was beneath ours. The tenant of our room was entitled to share the bathroom with the tenant—and, more pertinently, the wife of the tenant—in his room, and he decided there could be no safer choice than us, his neighbors and fellow villagers. The rent was twenty pounds a month with a thousand up front and the Doctor and I, along with a couple of other guys from the village, took it.

It was exactly four meters across and we each had three-quarters of a meter to ourselves (disregarding my piles of books for the moment), a figure that shrank whenever a contingent from the village descended on us and grew when one of us returned to the village. I gave considerable thought to ways of displaying my library, which was about five hundred books and magazines all told. I use the word display advisedly. I didn't stack them; I proudly displayed them.

The opportunity to spy on the neighbors made the window extremely popular with guests. The street was no more than two meters wide and its appeal went beyond our neighbors' sexual performance. There were, more importantly, the two balconies. The first belonged to the daughter of the Palestinian plasterer and the second to Hanan and Abir. Every single of one of us, without exception, had tried with all three of them at one time or another.

The mat was common property. It was the first domestic purchase we made in Ain Shams: white stripes on a blue background. It sat directly beneath the window. My books, of course, were not up for debate. Everyone agreed that it was only right and proper they be shown to guests. The gas stove, the bucket, and the can of gas were scattered about according to no recognizable system or wherever they had been put by the last person to use them. The washbasin in particular would never stay in one place for long. It served a dual function: officially it was for doing the laundry, but secretly it accommodated the Doctor's bodily relief. Lest the Doctor be wrongfully impugned I should explain. We all found the situation unsatisfactory. In the village there was lots of wasteland and you could relieve yourself anywhere you liked. All you had to do was lift up your gallabiya. Many nights were spent traipsing between the toilet and the room. The room was on the third floor and the bathroom was in the stairwell. As soon as I pulled my blanket over myself I would be overwhelmed by a need to urinate. Down I went, back I climbed, and so on. The Doctor, quicker to adapt than the rest of us, solved the problem. At first he spent the night between his bed and the bathroom, but the washbasin danced before his eyes, a shortcut to deep sleep. By the end he was using it regularly, every night experimenting with new ways to suppress the sound of his gushing flow. He'd place the basin between his feet on the edge of the mat, pause for an instant, then let himself go. Droplets would fly out of his control and fleck our exposed fingers. Some of us, especially the guests, would revolt, and before dawn broke they would've scoured the basin clean (scrubbed three times as prescribed by Islamic law), but the Doctor's persistence would defeat them. They were forced to add the spray and stink of urine to the list of woes to be borne when a man lived away from home.

Of course we could easily have augmented the furniture in the room with a bed and some chairs, or even a little desk for myself. The money we got from Mi'allim Matar and the rest was more than able to accommodate such demands on our pockets. But then again, it wasn't a permanent home. It was a limbo, a station platform that would either take us on to the life we dreamed of in the capital or return us to the village.

Whether there in Abu Antar's house, or walking the streets we would hide the fact that we worked in construction. We would leave in the morning in clean, pressed clothes, our hair carefully combed, and return in the evening the same way. As far as clothes went we were the cleanest young men not just in Abu Antar's building, but in the whole district. We would rise at six and descend, one after another, to the bathroom, then it was out to Salim's café in Shubra to catch the crew bosses before they left at eight.

The Crew

Matar's crew relied heavily on the element of surprise. I don't ever recall entering a building through the front door when I worked with him. He'd dig foundations and raise columns on any empty plot of land he came across. We'd always work on buildings about to collapse. During holidays for the employees of local municipalities we worked long hours. Friday was double wages: a day and a night. We'd ease the red wax away with a delicacy befitting its official status and work on until morning. But from time to time we'd work in inhabited buildings, buildings that were essentially sound but whose owners were worried for their safety or had decided to undertake renovations. The days of the Sheikh Ramadan project were a golden age for us workers. We would work practically under the feet of families. The project was an extension of the Sheikh Ramadan residential blocks. The buildings were surrounded by narrow strips of garden at whose expense the residents had decided, pretty much unanimously, to enlarge their apartments. After much thought it had become clear to them that the gardens were of no importance. We dug two foundations under each block and set up two columns, enough to add a meter and a half to the apartments. I worked hard and enthusiastically, coming straight from Ain Shams and foregoing my usual stop at Salim's café. We'd have lunch with the residents. Matar had made them agree to feed us when he was negotiating the contract. He occasionally performed this service, telling clients we were far from home and broke and it would be no crime to spare us a morsel. Food of every kind and, now and then, pretty girls to bring us tea and banter.

I worked a month per block, smashing up the balconies to make way for the columns. From day one I made sure to let the residents, and the girls in particular, know who I really was. I'd gently let slip that I had qualifications and even wrote for the papers when the mood took me. Circumstances conspired to help me. I'd recently had a story published in *al-Misaa*, so naturally I managed to place a copy of the paper in plain view. With great modesty I then informed one and all that I was the author.

The house was four stories high, its corners finished with carved stone blocks, and it had been built in the early years of the twentieth century. It wasn't in great shape. Matar, as was his wont, had deceived the residents into letting him hijack it, repairing it while secretly rebuilding it. For Matar, a dilapidated house resembled nothing so much as a venerable and serene codger hastening toward his appointed end, to whom surgery would grant not only a graceful and peaceful exit but also hope of a life to come. Extracting the dead from the living and the living from the dead: something like that. He never made the slightest attempt to imitate the style of the buildings he worked on. He occasionally added a few floors for show, but all the while the pickaxes were being unsheathed.

"There's no time." The municipality issued a final order for renovation. This was precisely what the mi'allim and his crew specialized in, and therein lay his danger: neither a repair contractor nor a building contractor but both simultaneously. Matar was a contractor, an engineer, and a property magnate, a man renowned throughout Shubra and the surrounding neighborhoods.

Hair like . . . like what? Like a snowy knoll, brushed carefully back off his brow and divided in the dead center by a wide parting, itself the product either of its extreme softness or a scarcity that suggested an impressive bald spot was in the offing. In any case his self-consciousness about the parting provided Matar with an acceptable excuse to keep patting his head.

He was always dressed in a suit and tie, necessary for his constant trips to government offices and, occasionally, to the police station. His face virtually gave off sparks. But what's with this "virtually"? It literally gave off sparks, especially when it was time to pay the wages and his face would sink back to the glass of Turkish raki. "Matar was an amirlay. That's a kind of officer, you know . . . ." Matar was busy going over the story of his roots. His mustache, with its color and silky sheen, was convincing evidence in itself, but he knew people didn't believe him. You could say he talked about his heritage with the persistence of a man who knows there are objective grounds for disbelieving him.

Matar had a simple strategy, starting by reinforcing the building. He would shore up all the balconies with wooden piles. Steel was too hard and therefore no good. Buildings, like the elderly, require flexibility, a little give and take, and wood can absorb their mood swings. The first floor balcony takes four to six wooden piles. From the second floor on up, three will do. Each pile rests against the floor, or alternatively is plastered into a corner, and supports the floor above.

The business of digging foundations only begins once enough time has elapsed to be sure that the scaffolding has adapted to the building. Each corner needs a foundation. They are dug out one by one, and it's slow work. The instant the digging is done, the foundation is reinforced with steel and the concrete poured in.

Getting the pillars in place is relatively tricky. The slightest error means a collapsed building. The building's corners, where the foundations have been put in, require skilled hands, good steel, and a tireless worker. Sometimes Matar would have to hire a mason, one of those guys who waits behind bundles of nails on Cairo's bridges. A space is cleared in the corner and the pillar is poured immediately. I would clear the walls and the Doctor would clean the foundation while the mortar mixer worked on the concrete. As soon as the pillars were dry prayers of thanks would be murmured, signaling the end of the riskiest part of the job.

A Visit

As I was revising the final draft the Doctor came to visit. He called me up and said he was in Isaaf; that he had just left Sanaa, secretary to Professor Ahmed al-Birri at the *al-Ahram* building. "Got any of the good stuff?" he asked and I told him I did. He chuckled. "God keep you, Professor," he said, "I'm coming right over." For a while now the Doctor had been following the progress of a philanthropic project initiated by *al-Ahram* for the express purpose of saving him from a court case over a bounced check he'd handed over as security for installments on a fridge. He hadn't paid and had been given a year in prison. His visiting me at just this moment I regarded as a good omen for the book. As luck would have it I was in possession of a sizeable chunk of hash, and I decided I would ask him why he had recorded the drivers. I knew the whole story. I knew that it was the reason for his eventual return to the village, but I couldn't understand why he had recorded them in the first place. I tried to imagine, or rather, to come up with some reasons on my own, but they seemed unconvincing and artificial. And here he was, the man himself. Strangely, he seemed positively enthusiastic, as if he had come purposely to talk about the matter.

He had eventually settled in the village and quickly acclimatized, transforming into a bona fide peasant: a Bedouin gallabiya with braiding on the neck and sleeves, a cashmere shawl, a white woolen headscarf, broad shoulders, and great rough hands from scything grass and dragging animals around by their halters. It became clear that he had no idea why he had recorded the drivers. More than once he said, "I don't know, I swear to God . . ." and he seemed to regret having done it. He said that he was still friends with Alaa, who continued to put in a good word for him with the bashmuhandis. Maybe it was some Ramadan craziness, he said, maybe it was fear.

It seemed that the actress didn't own the building, as I had imagined, and was no more than a somewhat hard-up resident. The actual owner was the bashmuhandis, Ahmed, son of the Minister of Tourism, a handsome, likeable fellow and living proof of the proverb "A duck's son is a swimmer." This duck's son swam and splashed about in a lake of tourist resorts strung out the length of Egypt's coastline. It may have been chance, or foolishness, or a shared predilection for possessions illegally acquired, or even their green eyes, but he and the Doctor got on from the get go. During the course of a little speech to the Doctor on the occasion of his starting work at the building the bashmuhandis told him, "The most important thing is cleanliness and keeping the residents happy."

"Right you are, sir," said the Doctor, who approached the bashmuhandis, eased his briefcase from his hand, opened the elevator door, and escorted him to the door of his vast apartment. The bashmuhandis thanked him and handed him a hundred pounds. The Doctor, accustomed to the life and style of a laborer, thought it was the new fifty-piaster note, and when he got downstairs and realized it was a hundred pounds he went running back upstairs. "You've given me a hundred pounds, sir," he said. "What did you want me to get you?"

"Don't get me anything," replied the bashmuhandis. "That's for you."

Delighted, the Doctor descended once more and from that day forward they maintained what might be described as a covert friendship. The Doctor was full of admiration for the distinguished, powerful, mysterious, and outgoing bashmuhandis and the bashmuhandis admired the selfless, devoted, and strapping youth. They were bound even closer by the commonality of their feelings toward the actress. Privately, the Doctor detested her overbearing manner, a feeling he expressed through knowing looks and gossip sessions with friends and co-workers. The bashmuhandis wore his detestation on his sleeve and the Doctor still crows about the time he gave her a dressing down in public when she'd called him by his name: "Address me as bashmuhandis when you speak to me so that everyone knows their place." She immediately corrected herself: "Bashmuhandis Ahmed."

The bashmuhandis lived in an apartment that took up the top two floors and beneath him lived al-Asiri Bey, with a whole floor to himself. According to the Doctor, al-Asiri Bey was an enigmatic figure. He imported and exported fruit and one got the sense he was backed by powerful forces. He came home every day staggering drunk and grew marijuana on his balcony. His wife was deceased and he lived with his semi-retarded twin sons and a beautiful but eccentric daughter. The Doctor said that she had once called down to him in the middle of the night and asked him, "Anyone with you?"

"No," he answered.

"Fine, then come on up."

The weather was cold and the Doctor ascended wrapped in an overcoat and narrow woolen scarf and stood outside the door.

"Come in," she said.

"'Come in' why?" he said. "Do you need anything? Because I've left the door open downstairs."

"Just come in," she said, "And we'll talk inside. I'm alone . . . ."

He simply stood there, baffled, and only came to when she started screaming in his face: "Fuck off downstairs! Get downstairs! I don't want anything, you animal!"

It was the night Alaa and the drivers had their party and they sat up all night teasing him for his naivety.

The building was ten stories on top of a warehouse with a large basement below ground. On the sixth floor, below al-Asiri Bey, lived Farid Rami, son of the celebrated poet. He was an old man of about seventy and owned a considerable fortune and a number of apartments in various parts of town. He lived with a diminutive and pretty dancer who put on daily shows in the clubs and casinos. He shared her with a young Upper Egyptian man by the name of Sayyid. Sayyid was her urfi husband and he, Farid, was her official husband, and both—in their own way—pimped her out to relatives, friends, and clients. Each was aware that the other was putting her to work, and preserved a delicately balanced unspoken understanding that allowed them to maintain the semblance of a normal life together in the same building: the respectable bey, his wife the artiste, and Sayyid the driver. When the Doctor first came to work in the building the three would fight with each other. He could hear them carrying on from the street outside the building. The poet's son insisted that she divorce Sayyid the driver, and of course the driver seized the opportunity, refusing to agree unless the bey handed over one of his apartments in Muqattam. He got it for the knock-down price of twelve thousand pounds, payment up front, and divorced her.

Two people lived beneath them. The first was Hani al-Husseini, an elegant, fashionable, and generous bey who was head of the stock exchange's board of directors. He was famous and sometimes appeared on television. He was firm friends with the bashmuhandis and al-Asiri Bey, and the three of them would bond over their loathing of the actress and the pleasure of belittling her. Although she owned two floors of the building and a fleet of the very latest cars they treated her like the dregs of society.

Hani lived on his own, though he was always being visited by his son, the only offspring of a failed marriage. He also had a beautiful lady companion who came around twice a week. Opposite him lived Dimitri Bey, a cautious, orderly man who owned a shipping company where the Doctor found work for many young men from the village.

The Doctor worked as a "boy," or assistant, for the doorman Abdu Sweilam, who, contrary to what I believed, was not from Aswan but from al-Idwa in the Fayoum. He was the overseer and connoisseur of the working girls, never happier than when all the beds were occupied. He'd smoke a couple of joints and sit on the bench in front of the building, eyes red, his grinning mouth disclosing gums of deep vermilion, and one leg draped over the other so that his gallabiya crept up to reveal a gaping hole in his trousers. On his head, like any self-respecting doorman, he wore a large skullcap.

In the beginning the Doctor devoted himself to the work. Up at five, pulling on the jeans and the shirt that stretched over his belly, throwing the rag over his shoulder and grabbing the bucket, he'd busy himself washing cars until eight, then run errands for the residents until eleven. He let the maids know from the outset that the time for errands was eight to eleven. If they wanted anything after that they had to order it themselves from the shop. Then he slept from eleven to five in the afternoon.

This was the time of day that Abdu the doorman set aside for the low-grade girls who came to the building from places like Musturud and Saft al-Laban. They'd do business with the doormen and laborers in the neighborhood and the drivers from the bus stop around the corner.

The girls would drop in at the market and putter around for a bit then move on to the building with a spring in their step. They would sit, three or four at a time, like a kind of shop-window display on the bench outside the building. When its owner the bashmuhandis came down unexpectedly and asked who they were Abdu said, "Sir, they're maids who've come to serve the residents," and that was the end of the matter. In fact the bashmuhandis was so affected by this tale he gave Abdu a sum of money to divide between them, but Abdu placed it emphatically in his own pocket.

The party began at six in the senior driver's room with the fashionable, flirtatious girls from Kilo 4½ and al-Darrasa. They used the building as a resthouse: they'd leave on a job then come back when they were done. One of the girls once went to work somewhere else, was caught with a Libyan, and sentenced to a year in prison. So for the sake of the building they placed themselves at the disposal of Abdu and his guests from six until eleven, then it was down to the street and the clients in their cars for the rest of the night. Two stood outside the Palestine Hospital and two on al-Saa Square in al-Nozha. Everyone in the neighborhood knew who they were. The work was all spur of the moment. If one of the girls ended up with a guy who had nowhere to go, Abdu would jump up and run to open the basement.

Naturally, the Doctor noticed and asked about the brutal noises coming from the basement. Abdu gave him to understand he was providing a humanitarian service: "Some guy and his wife arguing. They want to divorce. God help them through this little session."

But the Doctor went down and found neither husband nor wife but rather a decrepit old man atop a young girl no older than his own daughter. As he attacked them with a wooden stick the Doctor naturally assumed they would take to their heels. So he was somewhat taken aback when the girl shot him a scornful look and the man addressed him in a firm and confident tone: "You trying to rip me off or what?

I've given Abdu ten pounds so why don't you take five and fuck off?" before resuming his labors as if nothing had happened. So the Doctor had to swallow it. He left the basement as if nothing had happened. Abdu was his gateway to a life of ease, his immediate superior, and he was generous: showering him with food and drink and loans with no interest charged. He just wanted him to be happy in his work and asked nothing more than that he wipe the cars down and run errands for the residents when they asked. Things at the building were going swimmingly, everyone was grateful for the bright-eyed, obedient new assistant doorman, and anyway he'd come to work, not to put the world to rights.

Nevertheless, he resolved to keep to himself and to his work. He prayed at the mosque and got himself a long rosary of huge, fringed beads and spent the day fingering them and muttering invocations. Naturally, people began to complain about his hanging back to pray and his smugness, and the way he acted like a solitary angel beset by demons only provoked them. The actress would sometimes wait for him to get back from prayers and angrily berate him: "Has this Paradise of yours closed or something? I asked for you and they told me Your Worship was praying. Tell me then, is Paradise still open or has it closed?"

It was around this time that Iman first appeared, the extraordinary Iman to whom I lost my virginity. A young woman in her twenties, she stopped at the building on her way to an interview at a private company in Heliopolis and asked the Doctor if she could have a glass of water and rest for a moment on the bench. She told him about the company and her qualifications and how badly she needed the work, and he told her about the building and all the important people who lived there and the story of his leaving the village to work in Cairo. After that she made a point of dropping by whenever she could, every day a different excuse. The Doctor was delighted and fell in love with her: true love. He saw her as the girl of his dreams and started planning for marriage. One evening she came to visit and asked to use the lavatory in the basement. He got the feeling she was undressing and followed her, and there she was, throwing her clothes, item by item, over the bathroom wall. By this stage, their relationship was at a fever pitch of excited chatter, winks, and accidental contact, so the Doctor didn't hesitate. He strode into the bathroom and after a brief resistance she fell into his arms. He carried her naked to his room in the storehouse and as soon as he had her lying on the bed, in walked Abdu the doorman, who, before the Doctor had a chance to realize what was going on, declared, "God Almighty! You're up I see. Well, I'll just close the door and leave you to it." A profound sense of gratitude toward the doorman took root in the Doctor's heart—a good man, he thought to himself, the very best; a sensitive soul who had recognized his love for this girl—and, the atmosphere now rendered more conducive, he began caressing her. Suddenly, Alaa the chauffeur entered, said, "Evening, Doctor. Stay right there, I'm off," and left the room. "Don't stop," said the girl, to which the Doctor despairingly replied, "How can I carry on?" But he quickly pulled himself together and carried on, with her and her sister and the rest of the women in the building, and became a regular member of the evening gatherings with the drivers and whatever women they could get their hands on.

However he didn't abandon his prayers or the rosary with the big beads. He'd finish up with the girl as quickly as he could to catch the prayers at the mosque, and was constantly terrified that they'd be raided by the law or that one of the girls (especially that tramp who'd screw ten men a night) might die or that they'd do something to him, like his predecessor, who had been framed for theft after he fought with Alaa. To be honest, it's not clear whether they framed him or he framed himself. He arrived at the building a pure and innocent young lad and worked as assistant to Abdu the doorman. He began a relationship with the actress's maid. She would come down to the garage and he would go up to the actress's apartment. One day, following a fight with Alaa, the actress was burgled. She placed calls to the great and good of Egypt and the maid confessed. She said that she was working with him. The stolen property was returned and it should have been sent to the police for examination, but nobody called the police. They simply decided that he had robbed the apartment and he was responsible for returning the stolen property as soon as he could, then they threw him out of the building. For a while after that the bashmuhandis found him work at his villa in al-Muqattam, but ended up setting the enormous savage dogs that he bred there onto the poor fellow and they ripped him to pieces.

It was in such circumstances that the idea of a tape, something the Doctor could use against them if they turned on him, first came to him. Perhaps it was the atmosphere peculiar to Ramadan that helped crystallize this idea and bring it to fruition. He recorded a tape of drunkenness and debauchery, and worst of all, of stories about the actress and the bashmuhandis and the other big guns in the building, and who knows, perhaps in the whole of Egypt. The next day he waited for them in the room, Alaa's room, and when they started getting ready for their usual orgy he said in a loud, firm voice, "It's over. No more parties from today." They looked at each other in astonishment and one of them, laughing, asked him, "And why is that, Your Worship?" He held out the tape like a burnished blade and said, "Listen to this. I've got lots of copies and this one's for you." They didn't need to hear much before every one of them was outlining a different grisly end for the Doctor. "I'll flatten you with a car in front of the building," and "You're not even worth the two bullets I'm going to put through your heart . . . ."

But Alaa was having none of it. "The tape was recorded in my room," he said, "I'm responsible for it. If you want something from the Doctor you'll have to come to me." The Doctor relaxed. Feeling that he was now safe from death he decided to throw himself upon their mercy. He swore to them that he had no other copies of the tape, and weirdly enough he was telling the truth. In his eagerness to confront them and his careful consideration of the consequences he had neglected basic procedure. The next morning he received their final verdict from Alaa: collect your Ramadan bonus in full and leave the building immediately.

The Matter Requires Careful Consideration

I happened to read the biography of this foreign writer whose work I had never read a word of previously, though his name was frequently mentioned in the literary circles I moved in. An extremely hard life. He worked jobs that seemed horrendous even to a laborer like myself, but, as the translator emphasized, they "influenced his creative endeavors, left him enough to enjoy his old age and most importantly, demonstrated that he had first to carve away at the coal-face before he could achieve literary distinction." I pondered my literary distinction: a daydream from which I returned with all thoughts of the author and his life story and his trials and tribulations quite forgotten. I lifted my sack of sand and staggered to the stairs.

We were preparing sand, gravel, and cement for a house that Mi'allim Matar had agreed to repair and rebuild, or rebuild and repair, or rebuild while he repaired it . . . . Sorry. Anyway, it was an old house, very similar to the houses you find in Old Cairo: tall windows, wide balconies, lots of ornamentation, and a pile of old clothes and mattresses that Matar took as sufficient excuse to deduct a pound a day from our wages: "Sleep like kings instead of at that shack at Abu Antar's."

There were four of us—the Doctor, myself, and a couple of guys from the village—and Abu Antar's "shack" wasn't a shack, it was a room like any other. A door, some windows, and my books, it was something to be proud of, but we all felt the same way about Matar's proposal: the house, dilapidated though it might be, was still a house, and furthermore, a house in the heart of Shubra. We would be living there for a long time, for an eternity, erasing it from existence and bringing it back once more.

The storage box lay under a bed. One of them had a quick rummage around inside but found only books. He handed them to me in disgust. "Take them, Mr. Author." The author's biography stood out from the rest by virtue of its size and cover, and I accepted my colleague's gift with a demonstration of appreciation appropriate to a serious wordsmith. My excessive joy was actually a chance for me to prove my talents. Situations like these were welcome opportunities for public celebration of my literary identity. I waved the biography in the air and my words hung heavy with disappointment at my co-workers and life in general: "This man won the Nobel prize. The Nobel prize . . . . Do you lot have any idea what that means?"

Matar wasn't so wrong after all. The benefits ran to more than a bed, a book, and some old clothes. It was a spacious apartment: four rooms and two balconies, one of which brought back memories of beautiful women in old movies. Shubra and the girls of Shubra: there are neighbors all around us and lucky breaks do happen. Each man chose a room to suit his needs and made ready for a new beginning.

The residents had moved most of the furniture—renovations are no simple matter—but what they hadn't thought to move provided a life of luxury for men like us. Velvet upholstered chairs, a complete dining suite, beds, a modern bathroom, a satellite dish, hot and cold running water, and our world was turned upside down.

This room was mine. When they saw the desk they acknowledged there could be no debate. I was on the lookout for an appropriate setting in which to write a novel. I wrote in the room, the one in Ain Shams, squatting on a box of books and scribbling anything that came to mind, but it seemed to me that a novel needed something else: a desk; wood and iron. A desk, at any rate, and a bed nearby. The desk for writing and the bed for pondering the results. The room promised a resounding beginning.

What am I talking about? What novel? Enough of these questions. They only lead to frustration. Let's stick with Aula. My grandfather Aula. He spent part of his life, or rather more, sharpening his axe, oiling his gun, and sweeping down on the surrounding area to rob and plunder and loot and kill, mostly in the company of Abd al-Hamid, son of his uncle Deifullah, and Abdin, son of another uncle, Saqr. When the government came down hard they would seek refuge in the guesthouse of their cousin Yasin Abu Mahmoud, friend and companion to Hamad Pasha al-Basil, with whom he shared the headship of the al-Rimah tribe and later, in 1924, membership of parliament. Now that—by which I mean his guesthouse—is a story in itself. I'd love to do a whole book on it. Picture it: a towering stone gateway like the entrance to a palace and behind it ten feddans of the finest agricultural land. The table groaned with food and its doors were always open to the poets and singers of the region, to its starving and needy, the lost and those looking to get lost. Praise poems and songs of scorn were penned within walls protected and served by guards and retainers. It was sacred land. Even the government didn't dare approach it. So Aula did what he did and hid away for days and weeks at a time and they never laid a finger on him.

One day he was out walking the high country—the endless deserts of the South Fayoum—with his trusty companion Abd al-Hamid and a peasant. They were starving, on the lookout for anything, when they suddenly caught sight of a merchant riding at the head of a train of five fully laden camels.

Ibn Deifullah regarded this as a divine gift. "Aula, its manna from heaven!" he cried. "Shame on you, Abd al-Hamid," said Aula. "The man's on our land and we should protect him." But Ibn Deifullah had no time for that kind of talk and put it to him straight. "We're walking up to him. If you're coming, come, if not, then stay out of it." He strolled up to the merchant, grabbed the camel's reins and gave them a shake. Not surprisingly, the merchant grew fearful and panicky: all alone and surrounded by rapacious Bedouin. "What is it, noble chieftain? What is it you want?" He searched around for something to give him. "Get down," said Abd al-Hamid sternly. "Get down?" he quavered, "Why should I get down, O prince of the desert?" Abd al-Hamid pulled hard on the reins and shouted, "I told you to get down." Seeing how this was going to end the merchant shouted, "To the death!" and pulled out his billy club, which he raised skyward then brought it down and split Abd al-Hamid's head wide open.

While this was taking place, Aula sat waiting behind a rocky outcrop with the peasant. On hearing Abd al-Hamid cry out he emerged, leveled his rifle at the merchant, and shouted, "Stay where you are!" However, the merchant, intoxicated or crazed by his assault on Deifullah, bellowed, "You want something? Keep your mouth shut or I'll see you off, too . . . ." That was the phrase he used. Aula promptly saw him off with two musket balls to the face. Together with the peasant he dragged Abd al-Hamid over and tied him to a camel. The peasant supported the body, Aula mounted another camel, and they descended to the nearest village in Beni Suef where they sold their booty and it all ended like any other victorious raid.

The merchant's family blamed the murder on some neighbors who were known affiliates of their enemies. They started lying in wait for them and hunting them down and they almost managed to kill one of them, but then some honest citizen whispered, "It was Aula Abu Raslan." It was open season on Aula. He spent his days wandering the highways and byways, and they could have killed him easily, but because they were of civilized peasant stock from Beni Suef they first approached his relative Hamad Pasha al-Basil. They rode up to Yasin's guesthouse in convoy, with the Pasha at their head. "This lot want to ask you about their man's blood," said the Pasha. "You've got one of two choices: either Aula and his men swear they didn't kill him or they pay the blood money."

Of course it was Yasin who would have to pay, not only because he was their leader, but because Aula and his family had nowhere near enough to pay a man's blood debt. Aula was summoned and when he arrived Yasin took him to one side and told him, "Swear you didn't. You've got to swear, Aula, and the kids who were with you will swear, too." Then he led them before the assembled company, confident he would swear an oath after Abd al-Hamid and the peasant.

The peasant went first. He placed his hand on the Holy Book and declared, "By the right of those that ask, I did not kill him or see who killed him." Then Ibn Deifullah stepped forward and placed his hand on the Book. "By the right of those who ask, I didn't kill him or see who did it." After him came Aula. He stepped forward, placed his hand on the Holy Book, and swore, "By the right of those who ask, I'm the one who killed him and those two were with me." Yasin nearly combusted with rage. He forgot he was in company and shouted, "You can't manage an oath, Aula? You rob and kill people and you burgle houses but you can't manage an oath?"

But I've stumbled. Enthusiasm drives me on, and I stumble. I can't find the words, and when I do they seem heavy, awkward, and somber. I like to write with humor. I like to joke. But I always find I've been too serious.

Anyway, circumstances were different. The room was just how I imagined respectable offices should be. The window looked over the street and you could lock the door from the inside. The desk promises much: now I can begin. The first pages are always tricky. I don't plan everything I write, but neither do I leave it all to chance. I'll try to get things under control. The right environment is incredibly important. Perhaps I'll unwind on the bed. The matter requires careful consideration.

Glossary

amm literally the word for a paternal uncle it is both a respectful form of address to older intimates from outside the family (e.g., Amm Ahmed) or an informal term of endearment, roughly analogous to 'mate' or 'buddy' in English (e.g., Amm Shehata).

Bahr Yusuf otherwise known as Lake Yusuf.

bashmuhandis a conflation of 'bash' (Turkish, meaning head or chief) and 'muhandis' (Arabic, literally engineer) though in the novel it denotes not a narrow technical qualification but is a semiformal designation of rank indicating high social status. It is also used in general conversation to indicate respect or to ingratiate.

bey rendered 'bek' in formal Arabic and like 'basha' an informal Arabic rendering of a Turkish title, in this case Beg, it is used in two distinct ways in the novel: firstly, as an inherited title (e.g., al-Asiri Bey and Demitri Bey), and secondly, to describe the upper-class clients of the better dressed prostitutes who frequent the actresses' building at night.

djellaba a thicker version of the gallabiya worn as an over-garment.

feddan a unit of land measurement roughly equivalent to an acre.

gallabiya the traditional dress of Egyptian men and women, the gallabiya is a full-length robe or gown tailored in a variety of styles and fabrics depending on the social status and gender of the wearer.

koshari an Egyptian dish and fast-food staple of lentils and macaroni served with a tomato sauce.

mi'allim a title and respectful form of address roughly equivalent to 'boss' in English.

pasha or in Arabic 'basha,' is a Turkish title formally bestowed on Ottoman officials and officers of the highest rank.

shisha or shisha pipe, a term for a hookah or hubbly-bubbly pipe and the tobacco smoked in it.

urfi a form of marriage that requires no officially issued papers, merely the verbal consent of the two parties involved before a cleric and suitable witnesses. Although the marriage is considered legally binding in Egypt it is widely regarded as a means for couples to bypass the social and financial obligations of traditional marriage while legally protecting themselves from charges of fornication.